Demonic Anthology Volume IV
A Dark Humor Short Story Collection

I0591643

DEMONIC CLASSICS
ONCE UPON A DEBACLE

Demonic Anthology Volume IV
A Dark Humor Short Story Collection

DEMONIC
CLASSICS
ONCE UPON A DEBACLE

Includes Stories By:
Carlton Herzog	Erika Lance	Jamie Zaccaria	Jessica Chaleff
JM Paquette	John Di Donna	Josh Pritchett
K Walker	Kim Plasket	Larry Griffin	Marta Špoljar
Mike L Lane	Robert P. Ottone	Ross Ellison	Valerie Puri

4 Horsemen
Publications, Inc.

4 Horsemen
Publications, Inc.

4 Horsemen Publications, Inc.
1497 Main St. Suite 169
Dunedin, FL 34698
4horsemenpublications.com
info@4horsemenpublications.com

Cover & Typesetting by Battle Goddess Productions.

Paperback ISBN-13: 978-1-64450-642-4
Ebook ISBN-13: 978-1-64450-643-1

DEDICATION

To all those reaching to get your work out into the world! The author's journey is a long and arduous path, my friends. Celebrate the small victories and always keep climbing the mountain. We're no strangers to love, you know the rules and so do I. A full commitment's what I'm thinking of, you wouldn't get this from any other guy., I just wanna tell you how I'm feeling, Gotta make you understand... Never gonna give you up, Never gonna let you down, Never gonna run around and desert you!

ACKNOWLEDGMENTS

As always, this anthology is a team effort. My part in this is small compared to the submission reviewers, the previewers, the authors who bravely submit to us, and the readers who just enjoy a simple, goofy and quirky read once a year.

Thank you to...

Karen for your tenacity!

Ryan for your insight!

Kim for your expertise in horror!

Erika for keeping me on task!

And...

Authors for dealing with a 2020 dumpster fire and still managed to submit and be patient as I ran late in getting replies back!

READERS BEWARE

Everyone knows the classics such as Peter Pan, Huckleberry Finn, and The Wizard of Oz. Have you ever thought about what would happen in those stories if they were written just a little differently... More wickedly...

What if Tinkerbell defended her love for Peter Pan, at any costs including her soul?

What if Huck's adventure took him down a more dangerous side of the river?

What if The Wizard of Oz was nothing more than a surreal nightmare?

The authors within this tome have brought your classic and time-less books back to life with a demonic twist only found in the Demonic Anthology collection. Expect a very different impression of the stories everyone grew up to love, written in such a way they just might be changed in unforgettable ways.

TABLE OF CONTENTS

THE RIP VAN WINKLE PARADOX
RIP VAN WINKLE

Robert P. Ottone

"**Y**es, I heard you," Rip said, pressing the receiver of the public telephone to his ear in the crowded bar. Truth be told, he couldn't hear the person on the other end, his wife, and wasn't particularly concerned about it. He imagined she was demanding he be home soon, or to pick up a chicken from the corner market or asking him for a separation, which was what he secretly prayed for every night before bed, after tucking in their terror of a five year old daughter, Audrey. "Give a kiss to the Little Terror for me, love bug," he shouted into the phone. That's what Rip liked to call Audrey, his "little terror."

"Darling, it's been a banner day for the boys at the firm, and we're just having a quick cocktail to celebrate. Who knew September in the year of our Lord nineteen-twenty-nine would be such a windfall for us?"

He blew a kiss into the phone, and promptly hung up. He thought he heard his wife beginning to shout at him, and decided it best to apologize later than discuss anything further. It usually was, anyway.

Rip walked back to the bar, rejoining the boys from the office, and resumed downing his French 75, his preferred cocktail of choice. Since his company had moved upstate, Rip found himself enjoying the mountain air, spending time with the boys at the only bar in town, Crayon's, and drinking himself to oblivion nearly every night. There wasn't much else to do unless one was the hunting sort, which Rip, most certainly, was not.

"Gentlemen, to industry!" Rip shouted, as he and his finance-cronies downed their swill.

As Rip eyed Sophie, the bar's resident waitress on the far side of the room, he realized that perhaps he was a kind of hunter after all. She was his type, or, at least his type before he got married, with dark hair, pale skin and pouty lips painted a slick red. He waited until she was done placing the table's order down and turned back toward the bar before he toasted her. She smiled and shook her head. Rip had been in every night that week and found an opportunity to flirt with the young lady, who rejected him each time on the grounds of him being married. That didn't stop him from some innocent flirtation, though.

"My darling, when will you give me the time of day?" Rip asked as Sophie returned to the bar, placing her tray down.

"Rip, it is a quarter past ten at night," she said, pointing to the clock on the wall.

"Sophie, angelic vision of my night's dreams, that's not the kind of time I'm talking about, you delicious bear-cat" he said, leaning over to her."You're drunk, Rip, and I must say, the gin does your breath no favors," she said, recoiling.

Rip furrowed his brow and checked his breath. "Apologies my love, take thy beak from out my heart."

"Are you quoting Shakespeare now? That's a new low, even for you, Mr. Winkle," with that, a new order of drinks appeared on her tray and Sophie was off, into the crowd, to make another liquid delivery.

"It's Poe," Rip said softly. He turned, drunk and exhausted, and placed some money on the bar. "Gentlemen, I good you bid evening."

Outside, Rip stumbled down the block, making his way toward the hills. He wasn't far from home. In fact, he imagined that if his wife wanted to, she could easily storm into the bar in her night clothes and drag him out by his ear. She never did, though. He chalked that up to her watching over Audrey. The tree-lined streets of the town nestled at the base of the Catskills was picturesque, albeit, boring. Rip understood that he would never feel truly at home in the area, and often desired a return to the hustle and bustle of city life. But his job was here. And his family, too. So he was resigned to spend his days making trades on the market, flirting with waitresses, and spending as little time as humanly possible with his wife and daughter.

He found himself quickly confused in his inebriated state and wandered, blankly, off the road and into the nearby foothills. The town was nestled at the foot of the mountains, however; the town itself was little more than a few stores and a slew of large, beautiful homes. A company town in many ways, but a company town nonetheless. When Rip and his family arrived in town, he worried that the area was like an old western boomtown, where, as soon as the fun of making money wore off (mostly due to the money running out), the town itself would vanish and the enormous homes the company boys all built would be left to rot or be reclaimed by nature.

Rip stumbled into a large outcropping of trees, and looked around, confused as to how he ended up there. The last thing he remembered, he was on the streets in town, stumbling away from Crayon's, and making his way home. Now, suddenly, he was in nature, the lights of the town visible beyond the branches and thicket of trees around him.

Feeling the effects of the gin and champagne coursing through his system, Rip stopped under one of the large trees and leaned against the scratchy bark. He yawned and felt an exquisite exhaustion unlike any he'd felt in ages. Slowly, he slumped to the ground, his hands resting in the cool, prickly grass, and his head slumped down, chin to his chest.

A moment later, everything went dark.

When his eyes opened, Rip was alone in the woods. It was daytime, so he realized he must've slept all night in the woods. His wife would be furious, and his daughter would probably laugh, but Rip was merely confused. The alcohol had left behind a headache so fierce and a throat so dry, Rip nearly vowed never to drink again. He rose on unsure legs, his entire body stiff and aching. He stretched, and noted for the first time, how itchy his face was. He scratched, and was met with great handfuls of hair. He had been clean-shaven just the day before, and now, a beard had sprouted on his face longer than any he'd ever seen. He turned, and made his way through the woods, the worst hangover in his entire life raging through his body. Every part of him ached. He was nearly through the woods, when he felt nature calling from his loins. Pausing, he turned, and unleashed a hellacious stream from his member that seemingly went on for twenty minutes. His body shaking, and drained of what he would imagine to be every drop of fluid in his body, his eyes began to tear and he exited the woods, the sun beaming on his face. He rubbed his eyes, and they adjusted slowly, the blurry town coming into view.

"Holy cats …" he said quietly.

The town was the town. But at the same time, it wasn't. The once tiny, barely-existent "boomtown" Rip was used to had somehow erupted into a sprawling, gray and brown-building filled metropolis. It wasn't Manhattan, but it also wasn't the backwater he was used to.

Slowly, he made his way down the hill toward town, images of the night before returning to his mind slowly. He smoothed his suit, which was impossibly wrinkled, and walked slowly, noting how smooth the sidewalks and streets were. And the cars."My god ..." Rip said, eyes wide as cars of all kinds and sizes made their way down streets, pulled into parking spots, and sped around corners. He checked his watch, curious as to the time, but noted that it was seemingly broken. He took a few tentative steps down the sidewalk, noting the clothes and language of those around him. He was still in his suit, but that wasn't what people were staring at. His beard bristled and flitted in the wind, and as he walked, he noted how long it actually was. It dragged a good three feet behind him as he made his way down the street."Hey man, nice suit," a voice called to Rip. Rip turned. He spotted a group of children. Thirteen or fourteen, Rip couldn't tell. "Any of you wiseacres know where I can get a haircut?"

"There's a barbershop down that way, gramps," the tallest one said. He had a metal headband with a spiral-looking design on it.

"Thanks, kid," Rip said, turning in the direction the teen was pointing. He spun back around, checking his pockets. He produced an empty pack of cigarettes and sighed. "Hey, by any chance, can you fellas butt me?"

The teens burst out laughing and took off on their bikes. Rip stood, confused, and continued down the street, heading for what he hoped was the barbershop.

A little bell jingled as Rip entered the barbershop, signaling his arrival. He jumped at the jingling, but was able to refocus when the barber, an old man with a snowy white beard much shorter than Rip's, stepped out from the back of the shop.

"Well, I can imagine why you're here," the barber said, looking Rip up and down. "Take a seat, son."

Rip's beard snagged in the door as he entered the shop, and with a wince, Rip pulled it free. He was thankful there was no one else inside, as he didn't know if he'd be able to handle seeing more strange outfits or being laughed at again by teenage boys on bikes. The barber at least looked the part, in his white short sleeve work shirt, a razor tucked in his sleeve.

"When did you blow into town, stranger?" The barber asked, throwing the cotton cape over Rip's chest, and draping it over his body.

"I'm not too sure, sir," Rip said, quietly. "Last night is a blur."

"Had a few too many, eh, friend?"

"I definitely got zozzled last night," Rip said, smiling."Zozzled? What's that mean?"

"Umm, 'zozzled,' you know … like I drank too much."

"Drunk."

"That's the ticket," Rip said, settling into the chair."You've got an interesting way of talkin', son. Now just relax, I'll have you fixed up in no time at all."

"No time at all," Rip repeated. As the barber worked, Rip listened to the radio in the corner of the shop. It played music he never heard before from artists he didn't know. The announcer, a gravelly-voiced woman, talked about events that Rip didn't understand, and places he'd never heard of. He didn't recognize names like Trump, Seacrest or Obama. Were they places or people? Rip glanced out of the corner of his eye, people walking past the shop. Women in skirts so short that even Sophie would be shocked. Men with bulbous bellies, wearing sunglasses and walking around, bottles of clear fluid in their hands. When they were done, they threw the bottles in green containers, which were next to blue containers, which were next to brown containers."Why are there three different trash cans?" Rip asked.

"Oh. You've never seen that before? Where are you from?"

"Here. I mean, here, originally, this area," Rip said, slowly.

"It's a recycling initiative. Green is for plastic and glass, brown for regular trash, blue for paper."

"Recycling?"

The barber looked at Rip, confused. He continued trimming his beard. Soon, piles of salt and pepper hair littered the floor in clumps, like small cats sleeping all over the floor. When he was done, Rip stared into the mirror. He still had the beard, but it was trimmed and cleaned up, leaving him looking more presentable. Even his wrinkled suit didn't stop him from looking handsome.

"How's that suit you, son?" The barber asked.

"Looks great, sir, thank you," Rip dug around his pockets, and pulled some money out, mostly coins. "How much is it?"

"No charge, son," the barber said, smiling. "We all need a little help sometimes."

With that, the barber patted Rip on the shoulder and walked toward the back of the shop. Rip smiled, turned, and headed out the door.

***

From the barbershop, Rip looked around at his surroundings. A few blocks down, he should be at or close to Crayon's, so he made his way toward where the bar once stood, and in its place, found a yoga studio. Inside, women were sprawled on the floor, stretching and contorting their bodies in a variety of ways. Rip stood on the sidewalk, eyes transfixed on the women inside's flexibility, and the clothes that more closely resembled a colorful second skin than any type of clothing he'd seen before.

Eventually, one of the women at the front of the room walked over to the window and closed the drapes, preventing him from seeing anything further. Confused, Rip turned and started back the opposite way, passing a variety of people, of all different ethnicities and backgrounds.

The town of the past was largely white, mostly Manhattan transplants, but now, Rip picked up accents he couldn't recognize and languages that were impossible to pinpoint.

He found himself instinctively walking toward his home.

***

As he made his way down the street, turning toward the road his house was built on. The corner lot, where it was the only house, with the remaining lots around it ready to be built, he noted how the entire block had seemingly been turned into one large concrete and brick structure. Confused, he looked around, thinking maybe he had the wrong place, but in his bones, he knew that was wrong. The building was large, but it was divided into various storefronts. Where his home once was was what appeared to be a restaurant called "Soup'r Crackers." Rip walked up the steps and into the store and was hit immediately with a variety of warm, delicious scents that recalled for a moment his wife's cooking.

He looked around the restaurant. Where his living room once was, a cluster of tables sat, and people ate, ignoring his entry. Where the kitchen was, a vast expanse of soups in metallic containers sat behind glass. He looked for stairs that would lead to his and his wife's bedroom, or his daughter's bedroom, but couldn't find them.

On a nearby table, he spotted a newspaper. Checking the date, he noted that eighty years had passed since he passed out under the tree. He sat down at the table and in a daze, his mind unable to fully comprehend his situation, began leafing through the paper. He was able to read most of the words, and silently thanked God that the English language remained largely untouched, however, he didn't understand much of the news he read. He recognized the New York Yankees, but didn't know the players' names. He recognized some of the financial companies in the business section, but didn't understand the technologies being talked about. The information was plentiful, but all of it was impossible to comprehend on anything but a cursory level.

"Can I help you, sir?" The girl behind the counter asked. There was something familiar about her, but Rip couldn't put his finger on it.

"This used to be my home," he said, softly, looking around, sliding the newspaper across the table

The girl behind the counter was cute. Dark hair. Pale skin. Pouty lips. "Your home? When? The thirties?"

"Close," he said, with a smile. He rose and stepped toward the counter. He fumbled around in his pockets for the change he tried to give the barber, and placed it on the counter. "Can this get me anything?"

The girl behind the counter, the thin tag on her shirt reading "Sophia," started counting the money. Rip's eyes went wide when he connected the name to the looks.

"Sophie?"

"Sorry?" She looked up. "No, Sophia, I'm named after my great-grandma, but not like, completely, her name was Sophie."

"Your great-grandma?"

"Yeah," Sophia said, nodding. "So, this doesn't get you much, but, I get a free bowl of soup during my shift, so, what would you like?"

Rip looked at the metal drums of soup under the glass. He pointed at the beef stew. "That one?"

"Good choice," Sophia said, ladling scoops of the brown, meaty stew into what the store called a medium, but in Rip's time would've clearly been a large. "Grab a seat, I'll bring it over."

Rip sat back down at the table with the newspaper. The other customers finished their meals and left the restaurant, leaving Rip and Sophia behind. She brought him the bowl of stew and set it down in front of him, along with a plastic spoon and large soft drink.

"What's this, whiskey?" Rip asked, staring at the dark brown liquid.

"Coca-Cola," she said, laughing. He looked up at her. "Do you have any whiskey?"

She laughed again. "No, sorry. I like your suit." She sat down opposite him at the table.

"Thanks," Rip said. "Have you worked here a long time?"

"A while now, yeah. Where are you from? I mean, I know you're not really from here. Not with how you talk."

"How I talk?"She smiled. "You talk a little funny."

He slipped a spoonful of the stew in his mouth and nodded approvingly. "This is delicious, you're an amazing cook."

"It comes out of a bag, but thanks," she said. "How come when you looked at me before and called me by my great-grandma's name, you looked like you knew me?"

"Did I? I'm sorry, I didn't mean to spook you or anything," Rip said, stirring the stew.

"That suit must have cost you a fortune," Sophia said, examining Rip closely.

"It wasn't cheap," Rip said, taking another mouthful.

Slowly, Sophia's eyes widened. "What's your name?"

He looked up at her. "Why are you looking at me like that? My name is Rip."

She smiled. "Get the fuck out of here. You're him aren't you?"

"Who?"

"You're the guy that disappeared a million years ago. The guy from this town. Went out drinking one night, cheated on his wife, maybe punched a bartender, and then boom, vanished into thin air!"

"I never cheated on my wife, nor have I ever punched a bartender, thank you very much!"

She leaned back in her chair. "You're him. You're Rip Van Winkle. I'm sitting with the man who vanished."

"Stop saying that, I fell asleep in the woods outside town, that's all," Rip said, feeling overwhelmed. "I woke up, and everything's different. Everything's changed. My house is gone. Everybody thinks I talk funny. My wife is probably dead. My kid, who knows what happened to her? Probably in an old folks home. Or dead, too, I suppose. How old do people live these days?"

"Well, that depends on diet, and exercise," Sophia began slowly, nervously.

"Forget I asked. Her name was Audrey. Is Audrey. I don't know. This is all so awful and terrifying and I hate it," Rip said, tears welling in his eyes.

Sophia reached out and put her hand on his wrist. "Hey, I'm sorry, I didn't mean to upset you."

"You didn't. It's everything. You say people think I did all those things. When all I did was flirt with the waitress and disappear into the woods. Why didn't anyone find me?"

"I don't know, Rip. I'm sorry."

He leaned back in his chair and wiped his eyes with a paper napkin."Did you say you flirted with a waitress?"

"Yes, but I didn't cheat on my wife, okay?"

"Did you flirt with my great-grandmother, you sly old dog?"

He sighed. A smile began in the corner of his mouth. "I did. She was beautiful. She reminded me of all the decisions I had made to that point in my life. I had a wife and kid at home. The wife was a pain in the rear, but the kid … the kid was alright most of the time. She made me laugh, the little terror."

Realization washed over Sophia. "What did you call her?"

"It was just a nickname I had for her. My 'little terror,'" he repeated.

"Come with me," Sophia said, taking him by the hand and rising from the table.

Sophia pulled Rip by the hand down the street, further down the strip of stores that eighty years prior was open land that Rip would stare at from his bedroom window."Where are we going? How about you just drive me to a cliff and push me off? Can you do that?"

"Don't be such a negative Nancy, Rip, come on," she said, pulling him along.

Eventually, once near the end of the row of stores, the duo stood outside a storefront decorated with all kinds of antiques. Rip looked up at the name of the store: Little Monster's Secondhand Objet D'art

"Wait …" he said, looking in through the window.

"Go inside," Sophia said. "When you said 'Audrey,' it rang a bell, but the nickname. Little Monster. It all clicked."

Rip looked at Sophia. "You look exactly like her, you know. Your great-grandmother. Just as beautiful."

Sophia smiled and nudged him toward the door. "Go inside, Lothario."

As it opened, the bell rang above the doorway. Behind the counter, an eighty-five year old woman looked up.

Her eyes locked with Rip's. The look she cast upon individuals entering her store slowly slid away into impossible recognition. Her eyes welled with tears and seemed to sparkle in the light of the store.

"Daddy?"

ROBERT P. OTTONE

Robert P. Ottone is an author, teacher, and cigar enthusiast from East Islip, NY. He delights in the creepy. He can be found online at SpookyHousePress.com, or on Instagram (@RobertOttone). His collections Her Infernal Name & Other Nightmares and People: A Horror Anthology about Love, Loss, Life & Things That Go Bump in the Night are available now wherever books are sold.

https://www.instagram.com/robertottone/

https://www.facebook.com/rob.ottone/

Secrets of the Deep: Beowulf Revealed

BEOWULF

JM Paquette

"Lo! We have heard tales of the Spear-Danes—" the bard began, deep baritone echoing through the nearly empty pub and spiking through the ache in my skull.

"NO."

My voice was firm, and the man stopped reciting immediately, taking a long moment to drink me in. I'm big, hence the bard-stopping, commanding presence, and my looks alone are usually enough to send people scurrying. If that's not enough, the huge scythe resting on the table in front of me does the trick. And, on the rare occasions that both body and weapon aren't enough, I will flash some of my true self through the cracks of this human body—some red glowing eyes work well enough, a hint of horns through my luscious brown hair, the flash of fangs along my lip.

"You do not wish to hear the tale of Beowulf, greatest of heroes and slayer of monsters?" the bard asked a moment later. His voice was pleasant enough, but my headache was not tolerant of songs at the moment."No," I said again.

"Is there another tale that you would prefer?" he continued, head tilted. He had focused all of his attention on me as the only patron coherent enough to engage with him. A quick look around confirmed the elf at the bar was passed out in a puddle of drool, the dwarf at the far table snoring with his chin resting on his chest, the barmaid sitting on a stool by the kitchen door, nose deep in a book. The bard's expression was friendly and helpful, a customer service smile. "Geralt of Rivia, perhaps, or Lancelot?" he offered.

"No," I said for the third time. "No tales. No songs. No noise."

I came to this pub to get away from bards telling tales, but mostly, to get away from the head-pounding hangover. I knew better than to go shot for shot with the fey folk, I swear I normally was smarter than this, but it was late, and she was adorably sexy, and I lost my head in the competition. Lost more than just my head, apparently, since I woke up naked and alone on the floor of a strange room with no memory of what happened since the fifteenth drink...or was it the twentieth? Damn fey. They look all sweet and innocent and then they steal your memories!

I was damn lucky they hadn't taken anything else, though why my left sock was gone was still a mystery. Maybe I had lost it some other way, and the fairy had nothing to do with it. I had abandoned the other sock as I dressed, tugging on my boots over bare feet. They would chafe my human skin, but it wouldn't matter much. The body was remarkably durable.

Except for fey-drink induced hangovers, apparently.

A soft sound caught my attention, someone clearing a throat a few feet away from me. I looked up to see the bard had approached.

The bard cleared his throat again, and I considered how such a rich voice could come from that average build, that ordinary chest. I gave him a deeper look, then understood. The bard had bargained something for the ability. I wondered what it was. A dealer in trades myself, I knew the signs.

"What?" I snarled, though I admit I didn't much mind the sound of the man's voice. As long as he kept it to a normal conversational level, my head seemed to tolerate it.

"You seem...like you might have a tale of your own," the bard commented. "I do write the occasional song, you see. I'd love to hear your story."

"Do I look like the kind of man who would share my story?" I asked sarcastically.

The bard looked me up and down, then settled himself on the bench opposite me. "You look like the kind of man who has a story to share," he observed.

"You always bug people when they want to be left alone?" I asked, but there was no menace in my voice. I was genuinely curious. I wondered if the bard had something else along with the sound of his voice, some kind of persuasive magic that made me want to like him. It would make sense to bargain for both—a voice alone was not enough if one couldn't convince people to listen with convincing words.

I once gifted a man with the ability to convince anyone to do anything with his voice. I say gifted, but of course, it was a curse. Abilities usually are. And such curses tend to last a really long time, longer than he expected, no doubt. Last I heard, the ability had been passed through several generations. I really hope the man appreciated the love of his life while it lasted, since he gave her up for the voice. Humans made such strange bargains.

"What is it you want?" I asked the bard.

The man shrugged, his simple white shirt and blue embroidered vest moving up and down in a smooth motion. Maybe the voice wasn't all he had gotten—he seemed too polished for himself. Then again, he could have earned the motion with practice; a warrior's training would do it. I considered his hands, the fingers calloused from the strings of his instrument, but not the palms as from swordplay.

"You must want something," I suggested, not intending to bargain here and now, but distracted from my headache and willing to try something different. It had been a long time since I bargained with a musician.

The bard leaned back and gestured for the barmaid to bring us drinks. I didn't say anything, but he must have sensed my discomfort, because she brought two cups of hot tea, not alcohol. There was a time when that would have infuriated me, an insult, but not now. The tea smelled delicious, spicy and redolent of cinnamon, and I knew it would soothe my aching head.

"Maybe I want a new story," the bard said, casually.

"Not my story," I insisted.

He nodded. "Very well. Another then. What story can you share?"

I paused, considering. "You began the story of Beowulf. I presume you know the whole thing?"

He nodded, confident in his knowledge. "All three parts: fighting Grendel naked and tearing off his arm, facing Grendel's mother in the swamps, and failing against the dragon."

"Of course," I agreed, "but do you want to know what really happened during the swimming contest with Breca?"

The bard's eyes narrowed. "Unferth challenges him when he arrives to fight Grendel, calling him a coward because he had lost the contest with Breca. And yes, Beowulf lost...but only because he was busy ridding the sea of dangerous monsters."

"So he said," I commented, my voice neutral, but with a hint of knowledge that I knew would draw the bard in."But Beowulf swam all the way to Finland! The seas are now safe for sailors to cross!" the bard added, clear admiration in his tone.

"Oh yes, he ended up in Finland," I agreed. "And some monsters did die." I paused, giving him just enough time to fill in the gaps with his imagination. "But you must know that's not the whole story."

"Tell me," the bard whispered, delight and eagerness in his eyes.

"And what will you give me for such a secret?" I prompted, reveling in this moment, always the same after all this time.

"What do you want?" he asked, and I shook my head.

"You know better than that, Bard. You know how this works, don't you?"

"Are you him, then, returned in a different skin to collect what is owed?" I had to admire the bard. His voice didn't shake. His cheeks had gone slightly pale, but nothing near what I would have expected from a human facing his doom. I had seen much stronger men weep at this moment.

I didn't make him wait long. I shook my head. "I am not," I assured him. I don't know what he owed his other bargainer, but I would have to collect immediately on my own bargain. The man might not be around long to collect later. "I simply offer a story," I said. "For a small price."

The bard pursed his lips, thinking. "A small price," he mused. "For a secret part of a story." His eyes lit up. "I will exchange a secret for a secret," he offered.

"What secret?" I asked.

His face grew dark, and I could see the man who would bargain his soul for his voice. "A name. The name." He paused, his voice dropping to a whisper. "His name."

I leaned closer. Names were always valuable. I kept my own name a carefully guarded secret, like all demons. We are all subject to being summoned by our true names, a ridiculous loophole for beings with such power, but nature gives everything a weakness of some kind. Something had to exist that could debilitate us completely to make up for our immense power, both physical and magical.

I sat back.

"If you know his name, you don't need me," I said. "Why?"

The bard sipped his tea, face crafty. "If I summon him with his name, I will lose the gifts he gave me. He would be obedient to me, but I have no wish to own a demon. I only want my gifts."

"And you don't wish to pay the agreed price," I finished.

He shrugged, then nodded, no guilt on his face. Humans were all the same, as eager to break a deal as they were to make one. I wonder whose name he had, and what I could do with such a piece of information. Secrets were valuable currency, even the one I was about to share. Beowulf may be dead, but details like this one were still useful. The Truth always mattered in some way."Very well," I said. "One story for one name, exchanged immediately."

The bard nodded, excitement flushing his cheeks again. I held out my hand, and he shook it once. The magic jolted through both of us, the bargain reached, and he put his hands around his cup again, sipping more tea.

"So," he said, "tell me of Beowulf and Breca and what really happened."

I leaned back, settling in for the tale.

"So you know how we get here: Beowulf wants to make a name for himself, and he hears about a monster attacking the nearby kingdom, so he shows up to help. When he arrives and boasts about his awesomeness, the king's man Unferth calls his bravery and ability into question, suggesting that the man who had lost a swimming contest to Breca could never hope to defeat a monster like Grendel."

The bard nodded, eager for the good stuff, but always willing to listen to another spin a tale.

"So Beowulf admits that he did lose the swimming contest, but only because he was busy fighting sea monsters."

"And swimming all the way to Finland, after keeping up with Breca for five days," the bard added.

I nodded. "And after that, Unferth doesn't say anything else to challenge him, and the contest is not mentioned again. But, there is more to the story that Beowulf doesn't mention here." I took a sip of my tea, remembering the man's face as he sat in his little faering, oars lost to the sea, rain lashing his hair, lightning illuminating the sunken sun-reddened cheeks; it had been the face of a man waiting for death. My body had gills then and swam freely through the sea, but the dark depths are vast, and civil company is hard to find, so stumbling on a creature that could communicate was a treasure not to be ignored. Besides, even dying, the man screamed hero to any who could see.

"Beowulf and Breca spent five days at sea, each rowing against the waves—"

"Rowing?" the bard interjected. "The story says they swam for five days."

I gave him an incredulous look. "A hero he may have been, but no man can swim for five days."

"A man who slays dragons could," he mumbled.

"A man who was slain by a dragon could not," I pointed out. "Your swimming is an error of handwriting and transcription. The earliest versions say rowing."

The bard pinched his face, not liking how I had made Beowulf more human, but let me continue. "So there he was, lost at sea, tossed about by a storm, certain to die alone, when a creature found him."

"What creature?" The bard had leaned in at this.

"A creature with great power over the water, a creature who delights sometimes in saving lost souls. A creature you sometimes call the Leviathan, but who is, in actuality, not that large."

"Like the mythological Leviathan?" the bard asked, disbelief in his voice, but slowly putting the picture together. "The dark lord of the sea?"

I shrugged, remembering the old names. "Not so mythological, unless you think Beowulf is also a myth."

The bard paused to consider this, and I continued. He could decide his own beliefs later.

"So the creature decided to rescue Beowulf, taking him to a small island where he could shelter from the storm."

"Why not just stop the storm?"

"The creature controls the ocean depths. The realm of the sky is another matter," I informed him, not enjoying the reminder of the limits of my powers. "After the storm, the creature offered Beowulf succor and hope, and a way to get back to the mainland. In exchange, Beowulf agreed to slay several sea monsters."

"Why would the Leviathan want him to slay sea monsters? Aren't they, well, his minions?" the bard asked, face confused.

"Yes, minions, and willful, deceitful creatures they were, especially the nine who frequented the North Sea. The creature had wanted to rid himself of them for quite some time, and this human hero proved the perfect vessel."

"So the Leviathan just let Beowulf kill the monsters?" He paused, then added, "So it wasn't a lie—he did slay all of the creatures in the ocean!"

I shook my head. "Not exactly. They were sea monsters, after all, and Beowulf was just a man, a hero, to be sure, but only a man."

"Did Beowulf gain special powers then? A great weapon to slay the monsters?"

"No," I said. "Beowulf never got close to the sea monsters. He stayed on his island." I paused for a sip of my tea. "But they died, and Beowulf told everyone he had killed them. And everyone believed him." I paused, letting the bard figure it out.

"So the Leviathan killed them...But why? Just for spite? Petty revenge on willful subjects?"

I shook my head. "Oh no. It was more than that. With the North Sea riddled with monsters, few sailors were brave enough to cross it. People needed to cross the waters to get to the New World. With the monsters gone, the sea was safe again, and people traveled, and explored, and conquered."

"So, you're saying that the Leviathan sacrificed his minions so that men could discover new worlds?"

I nodded, sitting back again. "And then deposited Beowulf on the nearest shore—Finland—over waters as calm as a pond."

"But such a betrayal!" the bard mused. "Surely the other sea monsters would be furious if they found out what happened. They would rebel against their leader."

I nodded. "Perhaps they would. If they knew the real story." I waited for a moment. "And now," I said, leaning forward again, "my payment."

"Of course," the bard agreed. He leaned forward and whispered a name in my ear. I smiled as I heard it. This was turning out to be a very good evening.

The bard nodded, our bargain finished, and he stood up, collecting his instrument and leaving the room. I could see he was eager to add this new detail to his story, and with his exceptional voice, he would spread it far and wide. Someday soon, a sailor would sing it on a ship out to sea, close enough for listening ears to hear and report.

Finally, I thought, the demon who had replaced me as the Lord of the Sea would get what he deserved.

JM PAQUETTE

JM Paquette hails from upstate New York, so she misses the snow, but not the shoveling, and now lives in Florida, where she hates the heat, but not the beach. She has an embarrassingly large comic book collection that is only shamed by her ever growing horde of cheesy romance novels, and she openly admits to being both a fantasy enthusiast and a roleplaying aficionado-both of which have earned her solid stamps on her Geek Card. She lives in Clearwater with her husband, her daughter, her rambunctious dog, and a cat who occasionally appears at mealtimes.

"THE HAND-PRINT"
THE BIRTH-MARK

Marta Špoljar

Aylmer drew aside the window-curtain and suffered the light of natural day to fall into the room and rest upon his wife's cheek.

At the same time he heard a gross, hoarse chuckle, which he had long known as his servant expression of delight. "You," he said — his own laughter echoed the servant's, though now with a sort of frenzy. "You have served me well! Matter and spirit—earth and heaven—have both done their part in this! Laugh, thing of the senses! You have earned the right to laugh."

On the bed before them, bathed in the afternoon sun, Aylmer's wife lay dying.

The road that took them here was a short one, a steep one, and taken with little thought and even less need. Aylmer and his wife had been married for scarcely half a year; they had not rushed into their marriage, though, and had known each other for a significant two months longer. The wife he had chosen for himself — she was a woman whose voice nourished his spirit and whose face haunted his dreams — her name had been Georgiana.

And though it was now by his hand that she lay dying, her consent to the treatment that killed her had been informed and enthusiastic. Aylmer would have therefore felt no guilt, even if he were aware that his wife was, at the moment, dying.

Yes, Aylmer would have been reminding himself — were he aware that he'd just killed his wife — it was a treatment she had undertaken consensually, enthusiastically so, and fully aware of the possible outcome. His conscience was, as far as he was concerned, as unblemished as his wife's cheek was about to be.

The issue at hand — pun not intended (though, were Aylmer aware, he'd have taken great pride in such a clever turn of language) — was the

20

following:

His wife was nearly perfect.

Aylmer had always known she was nearly perfect. From the moment he'd laid eyes on her, he continued being aware of her near-perfection. He saw her, and he knew she was near perfect; he courted her, and he was aware she was so close to flawless. Her almost-perfection was not missed by him when they exchanged vows, or when they had their first dance, or during their brief honeymoon. And even so, it was only a week into their married life that this near-perfection, with all its implications, truly sunk in for Aylmer.

Were she only uglier, he often later bemoaned. Were she only viler. Were she only a chatterbox, or lazy, or were her flaws only manier.

But she was near-perfect. And this proximity to pure perfection, this being within touching distance of heaven — it was bound, he feared, to drive him mad.

It was a birthmark, you see, a birthmark that plagued him. Well, it plagued her cheek, to be specific, but as her cheek plagued his bed, and her visage plagued his vision, it was of little difference. It was even shaped like a hand, the birthmark — crimson, small in size but large in effect, and pressed right to her cheekbone, under her right eye. Yes, it was really a handprint, and it felt so fitting, for every sight of it felt like a smack right to his face.

He dreamt of it, often. Of it climbing up her cheek, down her nose, into her lungs. Sinking, under her skin, into her bloodstream. Cupping her heart.

Sometimes it moved over, crossed the marriage bed. Sometimes it rested upon his own cheek. He'd wake, and feel it burning — many a morning Georgina found him scrubbing at his face furiously, pouring sink water down his throat. He'd feel the crimson mark crawl around his rib-cage, eat down his throat. Bungee jump on his uvula. He could barely sleep. He could barely look at his wife.

It was stuff of nightmares. And worse still, it was stuff of his waking hours, too.

He'd been subtle, and diplomatic, when he first brought it up. "That birthmark," he mentioned, over breakfast. There was a bit of an English sausage on his fork, which he waved around casually (he was, you see, a man of worldly tastes). "Ever thought of removing it?"

His wife, sensitive as she was, burst into tears.

He noticed a change in her thereafter. He'd stumble out of bed, after a nightmare, and find her already in the bathroom; her hand would be pressed to her cheek, and her eyes would be full of tears. She started avoiding mirrors. She started only turning her unblemished side to him. And she only grew worse with every comment he made, no matter how gentle he made it sure it came off across.

Finally, as they were both nearing their breaking point, she asked —

"You asked me," were her words. "If I'd ever thought of removing it." She swallowed, then gestured, painfully blushing, perfectly remorseful, at her marred cheek. "The birthmark, you know."

He'd been staring at it from the moment she'd entered the room. It was truly impossible to look away from. "Yes."

"Yes?" she asked.

"Yes," he confirmed. They were eating steak tonight. He cut into it, precise and guided by reason. "I did ask that."

She was quiet for a beat. "Well." Her own plate sat untouched. "It made me think — "

His mouth was full, so he only hummed affirmatively. He reached for his wine cup.

"Well," she looked down, bashful and near-perfect. "I wondered...Is there a way to remove it?"

He would have kissed her then, were his mouth not full of steak, and were that long table not between them. And were her cheek not marred so.

And so it was that conversation that marked the start of his journey — the journey that culminated here, in this room, with the sun coming in through the window, and falling upon the woman on the recliner. It was a journey to save not only his marriage, but also his scientific career (because, in all honesty, it had been a while since he had last reported anything of scientific value and he was dangerously close to needing to go into teaching). He put his all into this voyage. He worked restlessly, without pause, without thought for long-term consequences.

And his dreams changed too. They were still repetitive, but that frightful hand was now replaced by a light coming down from the ceiling above him. "Flaws make us human," the voice coming out of the crack would say. "Why do you meddle with my creations?"

"Are you god?" he asked the first night.

"Obviously," the voice answered.

"The Hand-Print" by Marta Špoljar

Aylmer stopped asking after that, because he didn't like that answer.

"Stop," the voice kept returning. "No, I am serious. Seriously, no more vague sentences, I am telling you, this is not me being metaphorical, it is what makes her human. I repeat, this is — this is not an inspirational speech, it is that birthmark that makes her human. Leave it be."

But Aylmer had never accepted god as an authority, or women as human beings.

There were failures. There were semi-successes. The birthmark paled, but its shape still mocked him. "Get rid of it," his wife pleaded. She, for all the physical damage she kept enduring, had only grown more enthusiastic in their attempts. She'd straddled him that night, cheeks flushed and chest heaving. "Get that thing off me. Aylmer — kill me if you must, kill me, but just get rid of it."

Emboldened by the legal leeway this request had given him, he could truly put his all into the experiment; he threw all caution to the wind, and made moves no one else would have dared to.

And finally, he had a chalice ready.

The liquid inside it was silver. He knew it was potent, for it had already stripped all the varnish off every other vessel he'd previously kept it in. "There is a risk," he'd warned his wife as he handed it to his servant, so that his servant might hand it to his wife.

(He feared getting it on his hands, you see. He'd already burned his pinky twice, by accident.)

Her fingers seemed to ache for the chalice. "I know," she had said; her voice, the one that lifted his spirit so, had sounded the same as ever. Listening to it now, though, Aylmer could not help but notice an almost irritating color to it, a slight nasality. If this worked, he promised himself, he'd fix her voice next. How deliberate the universe had to be, he thought, how all-knowing, to pair this almost-perfect woman with the man who could make her truly so.

Her fingers grasped onto his then, and he flinched (he added blunter nails to the list of features of hers he would be improving upon).

"I accept the consequences," she said. She was staring into his eyes, or so he assumed (he could still hardly stand to look at her face; her almost perfect, yet so frustratingly human face). "Do you?"

He almost wept, then; almost fell to his knees, and begged for forgiveness. For almost-perfect as she was, she was kind, and humble, and put him first always — even thinking of how he would feel, now, should the experiment fail, and were she to die by his hand.

He considered explaining to her that she had given him her enthusiastic and informed consent, and that therefore, he would bear no guilt were anything to happen to her. He also considered adding that the experiment was so advanced and theoretical that initial failure was expected and that neither his name nor his career would suffer for it. Both his pride and conscience were safe; his wife was not, this was true, and he was not sure he would ever find another as ready to sacrifice herself for a greater good as Georgiana seemed to be — even so, he felt pretty alright about the risks he was facing.

He said no such thing. Instead, he said, "I too accept the consequences."

She smiled. "You do know what might happen," she reminded him. "What result this might result in."

The simplicity of her vocabulary, which often led her to reuse words within the same sentence, charmed him once again. "That, my dear," he said. "Is what drew me to science in the first place."

She beamed.

"So you are sure?" she still insisted. He had to restrain a sigh. "You are definitely, positively certain —"

"My dear," he interrupted her. "There is nothing my soul wants more than to go forth with this experiment, and see the results — whatever they might be."

She kissed him, then — he rejoiced at the contact — when she pulled away, she was flushed and excited, and she quickly took the chalice from his servant's hands.

"Bottoms up," she said, to the servant more than to him. He had no time to ponder on what this might've meant, however, for she had already knocked the glass back.

She fell over immediately.

And now here they were.

Aylmer was not aware of it, but the birthmark had already fully faded. Some had called it a cherub's handprint, in Georgina's youth — those people had been wrong, for the angel whose handprint it really was had been of a far lower rank. But it was a hand of an angel nonetheless — and it was the last thing, as Aylmer had been warned, the last and only thing keeping his wife human.

For his wife was not human. She was, instead, a creature of eternal damnation, whose desolation god had only managed to prevent by forcing her into a mortal body. So he forced her into a mortal body, all those years ago, and with a gentle touch of hand — officiated by a low-ranking angel, because god was too busy for in-person intervention — he then locked this creature within.

And the only proof of this having occurred, was a crimson birthmark.

Georgina had not grown up knowing what she was. It was something in the treatment Aylmer had given her, something in one of the early failures, that seemed to wear off the fog keeping her memory in check. How deliberate the universe had to be, she had thought then. How deliberate and all-knowing, to pair this almost-perfect prison, with the man willing to break down its gates.

I do not know, reader, what kind of a god did all this. I do not know what His motives were, either, and I do not know if they were justified. I do not know if He is a righteous god or a cruel one, and I do not know if this creature had once been human or simply a woman. I do not know if god is omnipotent and evil, or good but incompetent, so do not even ask — though that is a good riddle, I must confess, and a really good ice-breaker at parties.

All I know is, this god had defeated this being, and then sealed it safely inside a body that could bring Him no harm.

Until Aylmer excelled at what he did best.

He was warned, this is true. Aylmer was warned, repeatedly, and explicitly. It was his own actions that damned him, in the end — but when his spine gets ripped out, and his innards eaten, and his face speckled with blood as crimson as the divine mark had once been — well, this god will be more than happy to gloat.

The creature just waking up, on the other hand — and the pun, though it is still a good pun, is still not intended — this creature itself will feel no guilt for its own actions. It will feel Aylmer's heartbeat fade, and it will feel his bones crack under his grasp, but guilt? It will feel none, and it will feel even less of a reason to feel any.

After all, the creature will remember, as it sits up and sees the servant flee the chambers. After all, it will continue thinking, as it creeps up to its former husband, the man still laughing to himself. After all —

Aylmer had given it his most enthusiastic and informed consent.

Marta Špoljar

Marta Špoljar is a full-time student and an aspiring writer from Zagreb, Croatia. When not working on her degree in translation and literature, she can be found running social media for the Wondrous Real Magazine. Her prose has been published in Novel Noctule.

@shhhhhpoljar

mspoljar997@gmail.com

Careful, Wishes Are Dangerous

Puss in Boots

K Walker

One cold, gray morning, three poor boys returned home after saying one final goodbye to their mother. She had become ill, and though she fought as hard as she could, she was not able to recover.

Knowing she would die, she gave her sons the only things she had that were worth anything- A kneading trough, a pastry board, and a cat. Even the house in which they lived did not belong to them.

To the oldest, Tim, she gave the kneading trough. Terry, the middle son, was given the pastry board. Which of course left only the cat for the youngest, Trace. No sooner had the three reached home than Tim and Terry got to work. Though sad, they knew they needed to earn their keep. Trace could only watch in dismay as his brothers started working together. Troubled, he quietly retreated to his small room, so he would be sure to be out of the way.

So lost in his thoughts was he, that he failed to notice when the cat followed him, darting into the room before he'd closed the door completely. "Tim and Terry," he muttered, "will be able to earn their way, but what of me? I suppose I can eat the cat and sell his fur, but then what will I have? I wish I knew what to do."

The Cat, who had curled up on the bed behind him, saw an opportunity. "Do not fret, young Master. I can help you." Startled, Trace jumped up and looked around wildly.

Seeing no one, he paled, and whispered "Who said that?" Stretching languidly, as only a cat can, the Cat replied. "I did of course. Who else is there?" Staring at the Cat, wide eyed, an awkward silence grew between them. The Cat eventually lost his temper and glared at him, barely holding back a hiss. "Well? Are you going to say something, or just stand there catching flies?" Trace, who only then realized his mouth hung open,

27

thought that rather unfair, but closed his mouth anyway. He swallowed nervously before finally finding his voice.

"Since when do you talk?"

A sly smile crossed the Cat's face. "I have always been able to do so, though none of you ever cared to listen. You may call me Puss." Surprised, Trace spoke without thinking. "Your name is Puss?" His face clearly showed what he thought of the name, and it wasn't complimentary. Through narrowed eyes, Puss growled. "Well that was rude, but I will overlook it this once. I said you may call me that- I never said it was my name!" Realizing his mistake, Trace again swallowed nervously. "Oh... um... okay. A-are you... a demon?"

"So what if I am? You haven't answered me. Do you want my help or don't you? You did say you wished to know what to do... So? Yes or no? This is a one-time offer...."

Trying to think quickly, Trace considered as carefully as he could. Even if the cat is a demon, I need help. And he's always been a smart cat... maybe he really can help me. Seeing no other option, Trace nodded mutely. When Puss raised his eyebrow in annoyance, Trace hastily clarified.

"Yes! Yes, please. I'll do anything!" Puss, pleased, could not hide the smug look on his face. "Oh?" he purred. "Anything?" Trace, of course, regretted his choice of words immediately.

"Excellent," Puss continued, a hint of the purr still in his voice. "Now, I will need a pouch to carry things. Oh, and a pair of boots. You'll have to have them made for me, so that I may walk among the trees."

"Boots? But... you're a cat. What use do you have for boots?" Trace asked in confusion.

"What does it matter? Are you really sure you want my help? Those are the conditions. You can accept them or not, but you will not be having me for dinner either way!" Puss spat.

"I do, I do! Look, here is the pouch," Trace reassured, placing it next to Puss. "But the boots... well... those cost money, and I have none..."

"Hmm... yes, well then ask your brothers for coin. They are able to make a living. Surely they would be willing to help out their poor, baby brother." Trace hesitated, not liking the solution, but nodded.

"Good. Now, let us sleep, and you can ask them in the morning!" Puss continued with a smirk.

Careful, Wishes Are Dangerous by K Walker

Barely able to sleep, Trace got up the minute he heard his brothers getting ready for work. Stopping in the doorway, he called out to them. "Um... I was wondering... will you give me a bit of coin? I will return it when I can..."

Tim and Terry paused in their preparations, sharing a look of displeasure. Sneering, Tim replied. "You have your portion and we have ours. Why should we give you any of our earnings?"

"Well... Both of you have a way to make money and I don't... But... with a bit of coin I can hopefully change that." He could tell that neither of them really believed he could. Just as he was about to start begging, Terry spoke up.

I guess it would be the proper thing to do; he is our brother, after all." Disgusted, Tim agreed unhappily. "Fine!" Disappearing from the room, he came back with coins in his hand. As he handed them to Trace, he snarled again. "You had better not make a habit of this!"

"Thank you, thank you!" Trace shouted happily, quickly exiting the room before they could change their minds. Wasting no time, he immediately set out for the shoemaker, ignoring the strange look he got when he made his order.

Some time later, the boots were finished. Trace paid him, then returned to the house. Once in his room, he triumphantly presented them to Puss. Smiling broadly, Puss pulled on the boots. "Perfect! Now, the pouch ," he said , holding out his forepaw. Trace promptly handed it to him. Placing the pouch around his neck, and carrying the drawstrings so as not to trip, he headed out. "I will return by sundown with food."

～

Hmm... Now let's see... There is a rabbit warren not far from here. Those will taste good I think. I'll need to lure them out... Ah! Puss had just spotted a house, complete with a garden behind it. Easily jumping the fence, he stealthily made his way to the plants. Helping himself to some lettuce and a small carrot, he placed them into the pouch before continuing on his way.

Once he'd arrived at the warren, the clever cat laid down and placed the pouch near the entrance. Knowing he would not have to wait long, he froze. Sure enough, a young rabbit soon came out to investigate. Smelling the treat, the rabbit poked it's head into the pouch eagerly. Puss waited until the rabbit started munching, then pounced. The rabbit didn't stand a chance.

Examining his catch, Puss pondered. This is a mighty fine rabbit. If I bring it home, no doubt it will be ruined when the boy attempts to cook it... So, who do I know that won't have that problem? Oh! I know... isn't there some King in these parts? Now where was that castle...? Having a destination in mind, Puss set off once more. A few miles later the castle came into view. Finally! Ugh... way too far... I hate walking...Letting himself into the courtyard, Puss walked up to one of the guards on duty outside the door. "I have come to see the King! Stand aside," he declared.

Looking first to his counterpart, the guard frowned. "Who are you, and who let you in here?" he demanded.

Puss bristled. "Listen here. I've a gift to give to the King. What right have you to question me? Clearly annoyed, the guard sighed. "Okay, well, leave the gift here and I'll see he gets it. How's that?"

"Oh, no! I couldn't do that! The rabbit is a gift from my Master. Surely he would not like me to hand it over to a mere guard."The guard's face darkened in anger. "Now listen here, you- !"

But he never heard what the guard meant to say, for as it happened, the King's carriage rumbled into the courtyard. Giving the guard an impudent smirk, he darted over, stopping to bow a short distance from the door.

"Ho! Who goes there?" the lead/head guard challenged as the King exited.

Ignoring the guard, Puss addressed the King, quickly pulling the rabbit from the pouch. "Sire, my Master has bidden me to gift this fine young rabbit to you."Startled at being addressed by a cat, the King nevertheless recovered quickly. "And what is your Master's name, good cat?"

"He is called Trace. Duke of Fortuna, Your Majesty."

Pleased, the King nodded. "Come inside and dine with me, and then you may carry my gratitude to your Master." Puss's only reply was to bow deeply, which conveniently hid his gleeful smile.

Mindful of his new Master, he took care to save food for him, placing it in the pouch before saying his farewells.

Arriving back at the house, Puss paused as he heard voices. Loud, angry voices. Setting aside his pouch, he swiftly removed his boots and crept closer to the kitchen. Once there, he jumped to a high shelf, so he could survey the scene. He scowled at what he saw. Trace was sitting in a chair, across the table from his brothers, who stood over him. His head was bowed. The reason for their anger readily became apparent.

"I can't believe you used the money to buy boots for a cat! Not even for you, but your CAT!" Tim yelled. "Are you really that stupid?"

Now Puss, his temper flaring, felt he'd been insulted and he crept closer, ready to attack. But as he did, Terry shifted, allowing Puss to see the pastry board behind him. Puss froze. There, in the middle of the board, lay a lump of dough. Terry had clearly been in the process of shaping it, but now it lay forgotten.

Mouse! All anger vanished as he pounced, shrieking at the top of his lungs. Everyone jumped, none of them reacting fast enough to catch him. Puss landed squarely on the dough, but had failed to realize the board wasn't fully on the table.

His eyes widened as the board tipped, causing the bowl of flour on the other side to go flying. It didn't go far, however, coming to land upside down over Tim's head. Flour went everywhere. Tim yanked the bowl from his head, looking around until he spotted the cat. Puss, for his part, was calmly licking his leg. There wasn't a spec of flour on him.

With a cry of pure rage, Tim went for the cat. But he was no match for Puss's speed. He cleared the room in record time as Tim fought to get past Terry, who stayed put and tried to calm him down. Tim ignored him and glared at Trace. "Since your cat caused this mess, you'd better have it cleaned up before I get back!"

With that, he stormed out of the room as Terry wisely moved, but followed him out to try and help him calm down. Heartsore and worried about Puss, Trace set to work, hoping his brother wouldn't find him.

Sometime later, as Trace was just finishing, his brothers returned. Glancing around, Tim grunted. "Good enough. Now get out! And if you find that stupid cat of yours, it's not welcome in here!" With one last glare, they started their preparations over again. Trace, still worried about Puss and his stomach growling, made his way to his room, dejected.

On his bed sat Puss, the pouch lying next to him. "I brought you some dinner, as promised."

"What? But how?" Puss glared, and he hastily added "Thank you! ...but how?"Satisfied, Puss smiled. "You needn't worry about that." Seeing Trace about to speak, Puss cut him off. "It is not stolen!" Trace, who'd been about to ask just that, wisely held his tongue and kept eating. Once he was finished, Puss collected the pouch and both lay down to sleep.

The next day saw Puss in a wheat field. He'd passed a farm that boasted chickens and helped himself to their seeds, placing them in his pouch. Arriving at the field, he opened the pouch wide, propping it open on the wheat stalks. Patiently, he hid himself, and was rewarded not long after. In the pouch went two plump pheasants, which he promptly pounced on and brought to the King.

This time the guards recognized him when he demanded entry, and though they scowled, had no choice but to admit him. Today the King sat upon his throne, listening to petitioners and was quite happy with the birds As they were his favorite, the King gave Puss a ring from his own hand. Puss bowed low, making certain to say they were a gift from his Master, the Duke of Fortuna, then took his leave. On his way home, Puss stopped to snag two more rabbits, which he then took to a local cook's house. For the price of one rabbit, she made a savory stew, which he brought home for Trace.

When he entered the house, Trace was sitting forlornly, watching his brothers work. Once Puss presented the stew however, he was ecstatic. That of course only drew the attention of his brothers, who scowled, casting jealous glares his way. Trace, enjoying his meal, failed to notice. Puss however was watching them, hoping they'd say something. When all they did was return to work, still scowling, Puss smiled maliciously. So, for months, Puss continued his appointed task, enjoying the fact Trace's brothers didn't dare say anything. Then he overheard the King's guard's talking, and came up with a devious plan.

The next day, instead of heading out to hunt as he usually did, he waited for Trace to wake up. When he failed to do so in a timely manner, Puss took a running leap, landing squarely on Trace's chest. Trace bolted up, dislodging Puss, but, expecting the reaction, he only ended up in Trace's lap. Confused, and sleep befuddled, Trace stared at the cat. With a mischievous smile, Puss stretched. "Come with me today, and don't dawdle." Intrigued, Trace hastened out of bed and followed Puss to the river, where he stopped in dismay. Puss also stopped and turned to him. "Now, strip and get in." Trace paled, not moving as he stared at the rushing water.

"Move, or you'll miss your chance!" Puss hissed.

Trace turned to look at him. "But... I can't swim..." Rolling his eyes, Puss yelled "Now!" Startled into obeying, Trace removed his clothes, but couldn't bring himself to jump in. Puss, impatient, gave him a hard shove, then hid the clothes behind a bush as Trace fell. That done, he started yelling at the top of his lungs, knowing he'd be heard.

"Help! Help! My Master is drowning! Help!" he yowled.

Sure enough, guards swarmed the riverbank. Two of them jumped in, armor and all, to pull Trace to safety. All Trace could do was cough and sputter, since he had indeed been drowning. A third guard handed out blankets for them to dry off as best they could. Trace, close to finding his voice, turned to Puss indignantly as the King's carriage pulled to a stop nearby. Seeing that, Puss stomped hard on his foot as a fourth guard looked around in vain.

"I say, poor fellow, where are your clothes?" he asked.

Trace, more concerned about the pain in his foot, said nothing, giving Puss the chance to cut in. Waiting just long enough for the King to approach, he answered. "Poor fellow? Poor fellow? Why, this is my Master, the Duke of Fortuna! And as for his clothes, they're somewhere upriver! He was drowning after all."

As intended, the King heard and smiled brightly. "Ah, so it is you who has been so generous! I am glad to finally meet you, even if under such unhappy circumstances." Turned to look over his shoulder, he called "Gustav! Fetch the young Duke some of my spare clothes! We can't have him catching a cold, now can we?" A man wearing servant's clothing hurried to obey. After Trace was dressed, the King gestured to his carriage.

"Now then, won't you join us?"

Puss smiled, answering for Trace. "Thank you, Majesty! You honor us!" Trace, who had no idea what was going on, looked at Puss in confusion. Thankfully for him, the King just smiled and went to get back into his carriage. Puss waited until he was seated, then quickly turned to Trace. "Say as little as possible, you hear me?" he hissed. Then, not waiting for a reply, he pushed him into the carriage.

Trace ended up sitting next to a young maiden. The girl took one look at Trace and was immediately smitten, her face beaming. The King noticed and was pleased. "This is my daughter, Alana, young Duke. She seems to have taken a liking to you. I had almost despaired to see such a look upon her face, for all the interest she has paid to her suitors!" Alana blushed, ducking her head. Trace, who had barely looked at her, glanced over with wide eyes. Feeling foolish, he tried a smile. This, of course, only encouraged her. Having no clue what to say, Trace turned back to the King and smiled nervously. The King was used to that reaction though, and returned the smile, then sat back and signaled the driver to continue on.

Puss knew he could not remain idle if his plan was to succeed. So he gave a nod to the guards, then raced ahead. He had better keep his mouth shut. If he ruins this...

Soon he came upon some commoners, cutting down the long grass in a field. Their scythes gleamed in the light as Puss stopped in front of them. "Listen, all of you! If you don't tell the King this field belongs to the Duke of Fortuna, I'll cut you into pieces!" For good measure, he flashed his claws. Claws which lengthened as they watched. As their faces paled, Puss knew they'd obey and ran off.

Not long after, the King pulled up. "I say, good gentlemen! To whom does this field belong?" he asked jovially.

Fearful of Puss's threat, one called loudly, "It belongs to the Duke of Fortuna, Majesty." Impressed, the King called his thanks and they continued on. "You seem to have inherited a fine estate, young Duke," he said as he turned to Trace.

"Err... well, I suppose sir. This meadow never fails to yield a good crop every year." Duke? Why is he calling me that? Should I have answered? It didn't seem like a test... It's a good thing I always listen to the villagers in the tavern..., Trace thought, because of course he knew nothing of farming. His reply seemed to be the right one though, as the King smiled.

Next they came upon some harvesters. It was clear they'd already met Puss, as their faces paled when they caught sight of the King. "Good sirs, who owns all these fine fields around us?" the King asked as the carriage neared.

"Oh... 'tis the Duke of Fortuna, King sir." With that reply, the King looked almost smug. He nodded and they continued on, as the harvesters breathed a sigh of relief. Puss made the same threat to all he met and none even thought to disobey his orders. The King was beyond impressed by this point.

~~~~

Finally, Puss, a little out of breath, reached a fine castle. From previous experience, he knew a dreadful ogre ruled the castle and that all the lands surrounding it belonged to him, as he'd stolen them from the rightful Lord. Stopping outside the keep door, Puss looked at the scared man standing guard. This one he didn't bother to threaten.

"I don't wish to be rude and pass so close without paying my respects to the Lord of the castle. Please may I have an interview?" Puss asked politely.

The poor man, not a little starved, paled but nonetheless did his duty and entered the keep. Not a minute later and he was back, beckoning Puss inside. The guard quickly closed the door behind him, remaining outside. The ogre, sitting on a 'throne' made of piled cushions, smiled cruelly."And what do you want, little cat?" he boomed."Well... I was curious, you see. I heard you can actually turn into any kind of animal you want, but I can hardly believe that."The ogre, feeling insulted, roared. "It is true! I'll even show you, puny cat!" The ogre then changed into a snarling tiger and chased Puss around the courtyard, which he escaped by ducking into a crack in the wall. The ogre, satisfied his point had been made, returned to his throne and changed back.

"Well that was certainly a fright!" Puss proclaimed, as he returned to the front of the dais. This pleased the ogre, and his smile returned.

"Although," Puss continued as the ogre scowled. "I have also heard that you can even change into creatures that are surely far too tiny for one such as you. I would really like to see such an impossible feat, but this courtyard is rather... grimy. I'm not sure I would be able to see if such a thing were true!"

Sneering, the ogre looked around. It was indeed filthy. Anything small would likely disappear into the mud. Grumbling mightily, the ogre replied "Fine! But if we should go somewhere brighter, then I may ask you for anything I want in return, and you must obey without fail! Understood?"

"Hmm... I guess if you insist..." Puss agreed reluctantly. "Coming through the forest, I passed by a clearing not too far from here. Will that do?"

"Whatever. Lead the way," the ogre grunted, clearly annoyed. So puss led him outside, past the guard, who shrank away, and to a clearing he'd found years ago. One with a certain cave at one end. Puss felt smug as he noticed yellow eyes glaring at them from the darkness.

"Here we are! Now, I still don't believe you can change into a mouse," Puss said, stopping near the cave.

"Grr... I'll show you!" And his body began to shrink, until he'd become a tiny gray mouse. Seeing this, the occupant living in the cave shot out and pounced. Puss didn't move as he watched the other cat eat the transformed ogre.

"Ha! I stole your prey!" the other cat crowed. "Now, I told you a long time ago I never wanted to see you in my territory again! Did you forget what I told you would happen, stupid intruder?" Teeth bared, the other cat advanced on all fours, hair standing on end.

Puss watched intently as his would-be-opponent stopped, a strange look coming over his face. When a paw went to his stomach, Puss wisely took cover behind a nearby tree. No sooner did he get there than there was a tremendous SPLATT! The tree shuddered from the impact and a foul stench enveloped Puss. Covering his nose, he peered around the tree.

Yep. Thought so. What shrinks must return to normal when dead. Yuck. Note to self, avoid this clearing for a while. Running back to the castle, Puss heard the carriage drawing near. With little time left, he darted past the guard again, into the courtyard. Clapping his paws together, he smiled in satisfaction.

"Oh father! What a gorgeous castle! May we stop for a visit?" the princess exclaimed. Taking that as his cue, Puss opened the door, nodding to the guard before going to meet the carriage.

"Welcome! Welcome to Destiny's Keep, home of the Duke of Fortuna!"The poor guard, standing behind Puss, saluted the carriage, hoping the ogre was gone for good.

"What? This too is yours, young Duke? Well, then with your permission, may we look around?"

Trace hesitated, unsure, but a glare from Puss loosened his tongue. "Ah... yes. Of course," he said weakly. The guard, still playing along, helped the Princess out of the carriage on one side as the King and Trace exited the other.

The King and his escort followed as Puss opened the door to the courtyard. The resident guard's mouth dropped open and he gaped at the now pristine courtyard. Just before they got to the inner door, Puss gave them a quick smile and dashed through the door, slamming it behind him. Those following had only enough time to jump in surprise, before Puss re-opened the door and held it for them with a bow. Recovering, they dismissed his odd behavior and entered the Hall.

Their eyes widened as they took in the banquet that had been laid out. A long table in the center of the room was covered in delicious food. Mouths watered as each of them spotted a favorite dish. Eagerly, the three of them chose the seats nearest them and sat down, Puss holding the chair for the Princess. She of course insisted on sitting next to Trace. The guards fanned out, taking positions to guard the exits.

Puss, instead of taking a seat himself, acted as a waiter. He made sure to bring any food they wanted and never let the King's cup run dry. For the Princess, he served a weaker version of the wine in her father's glass. To Trace, he gave water. When he would have protested, Puss kicked him below the table and glared once more.

After several cups of wine had been emptied, Puss spoke up, hoping to start the conversation flowing. "You have a beautiful daughter, good King!"Beaming, the King replied readily. "Oh yes, good cat! She is the light of my life! Though I must tell you she has had me worried. Not interested in even one suitor. Not one!"Puss smiled gleefully, though even he hadn't expected an opening so soon. "Hmm… I have noticed she seems quite enamored of my Master."

"Oh! Yes, that is quite right! You are, aren't you daughter?" Her cheeks bright red, she chose not to reply. Trace was speechless, as he still had no idea what was happening. Puss has a lot of explaining to do…

"My good man! No… my good Duke! You are of good standing and own a fine estate. One of the finest I have seen. Very fine. So, I ask you, will you make my daughter happy?"

"Uh…" mind blank, Trace could only stare.

"What he means, Master, is are you willing to marry her? Is that not right, my King?"

The King, who hadn't actually meant that, thought it was a great idea. "Sure! That would be a fine thing! You will marry my daughter, won't you?"

"Father! It should be HIM asking ME, not you asking him! Alana protested.

"Oh…yes. True. But will you marry her?" he continued. At a loss for words, Trace just sat there as he gaped in disbelief.

Puss leaned in to whisper in his ear. "Say yes, you idiot!" Jolted out of his daze, Trace obeyed.

"Yes, you id-mph…" Puss had covered his mouth with his paw, cutting him off. "What is wrong with you?" Puss hissed. "Are you trying to ruin this?"

Thankfully the King hadn't noticed his near slip. "Excellent! So let us return to my castle and start the preparations!"

Invitations had been sent out. The wedding would be at the end of the week. The King had pushed for sooner, but his advisors refused. "Some of your subjects are several days away. You can't possibly think they'll all arrive in less than a day!" they scolded. Sighing in disappointment, the King agreed. All he wanted was to see his daughter happily wed and taken care of properly. She looked so much happier now. Happier than she'd been since the day her mother died.

He looked across the Royal Suite, where seamstresses were offering Alana a selection of dresses. The talk of this cut versus that style made no sense to him, but his daughter couldn't seem to stop smiling, and his heart lifted in joy.

Meanwhile, Puss had his paws full dealing with Trace. They had stayed at the ogre's castle, and Trace was proving to be stubborn.

"But none of this is mine, Puss! I'm no Duke, and I am in no way qualified to marry a Princess!"

Trying hard not to roll his eyes, Puss reasoned with him. "The owner of this castle is dead. He had no heirs, so why not you? Besides, I'm not going to let you ruin my plans. Not to mention the girl. Did you even look at her face? Do you really want to break her heart?"

"Well, no, but… wait a minute! How do you know the owner is dead? Did you… kill him?"

"Of course I didn't kill him! What do you take me for, an uncivilized beast?"

"Well… no… but… well what did happen to the former owner?"

"Who cares? I just heard he was dead, and you don't see him or anyone

CAREFUL, WISHES ARE DANGEROUS BY K WALKER

else lying around, do you?"

"Well... no..."

"Then drop it! The castle is yours, and if you're still not sure about it, you'll be marrying the girl soon anyway." He eyed Trace critically "Meanwhile, you need new clothes..." His voice trailed off as he advanced toward Trace.

"What? But these are perfectly fine! Why do I..."

"Those belong to the King, in case you've forgotten. You do need to return them, and your clothes are only fit for rags! Now come on! There's got to be some coins around here. Then we'll go buy some clothes."Trace almost protested again, but seeing Puss wasn't going to take no for an answer, he reluctantly followed.

———

One bright morning a few days later, the King's carriage pulled up to the castle. Trace, in his new finery, was waiting outside, Puss beside him. He'd wanted to run, but Puss wouldn't let him. He'd even made him sleep at the castle, in spite of the fact it stank. Puss refused to tell him why it stank, or why the smell increased whenever the wind blew from a certain direction... like now.

He tried to keep his face blank, but didn't think he succeeded too well. Even the driver looked a little green. Once they'd climbed into the seats, he pulled away quickly, leaving the castle behind. Puss pulled out a couple incense sticks from his pouch, along with a book of matches. Lighting them, he handed one to Trace.

"I wish you hadn't wasted good money on those, but I'm grateful all the same. I think the smell is actually getting worse. We should really go investigate..."

"I said no! Now stop asking. Think of the day ahead, so you don't make a fool of yourself! Have you been reading those books I told you to read?"

"Oh. Uh... yes, though it was slow going. We never had much time to read growing up, so..."

"Ok! That's fine then. Focus on what you read." Trace sighed, and the rest of the journey was made in silence.

———

The wedding itself was almost anticlimactic. Trace repeated after the Priest like he was supposed to, though he still wanted to run. Only the claws digging into his leg prevented him from doing just that, since of course Puss was his best man. The King had not been told of trace's brothers, so they weren't there. Trace kissed the Princess when prompted, his face turning beet red. What was her name again? Trace thought in panic. Oh man... I really don't want to be here...

The feast after the wedding was loud with food and wine flowing freely. It was nearly dawn before Alana made their excuses and pulled Trace away. Puss watched them go, glaring at Trace, almost daring him to run. For his part, Trace was more afraid of what Puss might do to him if he ran, so he dutifully followed the Princess. They did not get much sleep that night.

For the next few days, Trace got acquainted with his new life. The Princess helped him as best she could, even going so far as to hire tutors for her new husband when she found out the depth of his knowledge. Or rather the lack of it. Puss thought it was hilarious and taunted him whenever they were alone.

So the days went, until one gloomy morning shouts rang out, waking the whole castle. The King was dead. None knew exactly what had happened, or how, but huge gashes were found to be the fatal blows. Naturally, Puss was sought out, as the only one sporting claws, but it was determined his paws were far too small. No one was able to find the culprit, so they did the only thing they could and held a funeral for the King. Alana could not stop crying, and she clung desperately to Trace. Having no other choice, a coronation was held after the funeral concluded.

Trace thought it seemed disrespectful and wrong to hold it so soon, but he was assured the people needed to see a King on the Throne or riots would break out. Since Alana was the only heir, that made Trace the new King. He wasn't thrilled with this turn of events, but was now thoroughly stuck with it and running wasn't an option.

Doing the best he could, he listened to his wife and advisors. He thought he was doing a passable job, but of course he still felt like a fraud. Not long after that the new Queen found she was with child and the Kingdom rejoiced. She retired early to her rooms to rest. Trace remained in his office, and that is where Puss found him.

"Haven't had much time to talk these days, have we?" Puss asked by way of greeting.

"No... we haven't. I'm sorry- I've been so busy lately..."But Puss waived his apologies away dismissively. "Yes, yes. But that's not why I'm here. You see, it's time."

"Time for what, good cat?" Trace asked with a smile.

"Time for me to say goodbye to you, but first we must settle the matter of my price."

"Price?" Trace asked as his smile vanished and a chill went down his spine.

"Of course. You didn't really think you were getting all this for the price of a pair of boots, did you?"

K WALKER

K. Walker has always wanted to be a writer. She has a huge imagination, helped along by her love of reading and the written word. With the dictionary she carries around in her head, she also makes a good editor. K. has always wanted to spread her love of reading by writing her own stories for others to enjoy. She'll write about anything that catches her interest. Her favorite genre to write is fantasy and anything that makes her imagination soar, because there's no telling what will pop into her head. She loves to read Sci-Fi, Fantasy, Paranormal Romance, and even a bit of Mystery and Horror, but Non-Fiction books have been known to put her to sleep. Her imagination gets pulled in so many directions, her mind is pure chaos, so this is the first story she's managed to finish, though she hopes to one day finish the other stories bouncing around inside her head. She also enjoys spending time on games and will most often be seen playing League of Angels with her friends when she isn't reading, editing, researching, or trying to write down all the ideas clamoring for her attention.

EMERALD VIEWS
WIZARD OF OZ

Kim Plasket

CHAPTER 1

They came walking in again, I have no idea what possesses them to keep coming back. They come waltzing in here as if they own the place. I know the secrets of this Emerald City like the very back of my hand. Most of the time I'm overlooked simply because I stay in the background.

The secrets I could tell about this place and its inhabitants would be enough for you to gasp in shock. You see before you a wonderful place full of magic and majesty but I see the truth if you want to know just keep reading.

The Guardian of the gates met them and needless to say he was stunned since he knew they went to the Wicked Witch of the East. He expected them to become the slaves, I guess he was picturing the lion as a new type of bear rug or the scarecrow as fodder for her fireplace.

I wonder if the tin man could be a beehive or maybe a place for those winged beasts to hang out between jobs, either way, I'm sure she could figure it out. I guess the girl, I think they called her Dorothy, could help in the kitchen but that yappy thing at her feet well they would have to get rid of it. First of all, it's loud, second, it makes a mess all over the nice clean floor.

"What are you doing back here?" The guardian said when he finally answered the bell that had been ringing for a long time. I was tempted to answer it myself but the last time I did they told me I would be picking up sticks in the forest and after the last time I never wanted to go there again. I still had nightmares and it was over a year ago.

"Did you not hear us ringing the bell?" Dorothy said.

"You went to the wicked witch of the East. Did she just let you go?" he was looking at them in confusion because it was well known she didn't let anyone go once she got a hold of them.

"She had no choice," the tin man said, confidence oozing from his voice.

"Why not?" the guardian was looking around as if he was scared she would just show up at the door.

"She has melted" those words caused the guardian to look at them with shock written on his face.

"Who melted her?" he looked from one to the other.

"It was Dorothy," the lion said his voice nearly a whisper.

"Gracious" he bowed so low to her his head nearly hit the floor. Really it was overacting if you ask me.

Chapter 2

He took them to the room where the spectacles were, they were told the first time they came here that the spectacles helped them to not be blinded by the Emerald City. I was the only one who never wore them. At first, I was sad about it, but then I realized it was better.

I was able to see just what was going on, I knew if something was out of place or if parts of the building were breaking down. I could get someone to fix them, even if they didn't really see me they could see if I pointed something out but otherwise I was invisible to them.

After they got the glasses on he led them to the main gate, what a fuss was made over them. The guard happened to let it slip they battled the Wicked Witch, he told the masses they fought her.

"The witch had seen them coming so at night when the girl and lion were asleep she sent her wolves to sneak up on them, the tin man used his ax and cut them all up when the girl woke up she was scared but her friends assured her it would be okay." he began the tale as if the very existence of all depended on it.

"She was angry as any witch would be so she then sent her crows to get them but the scarecrow told them to lie beside him and he would not allow them to be injured. As the crows approached him they were scared but the king crow told his mates to not be scared as the scarecrow was nothing to be afraid of." the crowd was enthralled.

"Little did he know this scarecrow wasn't to be taken lightly, he grabbed the head of the king of the crows and twisted until he broke his neck. Each crow that flew at him he snapped their necks like they were made of twigs. The cracking could be heard for miles around, in the end, the only thing left was a pile of feathers and blood." the gasps were heard for miles.

"The witch saw the carnage and she sent her precious black bees to sting them to death, the group saw them coming from miles away so the scarecrow had the woodsman take his stuffing and cover the girl, the yappy thing and the lion so they were hidden from view. The only one they saw was the tinman of course when the stung him nothing happened to him but they all died." he was loving the attention.

"The witch was furious when she saw her precious bees scattered on the ground like pieces of coal so she decided to arm the winkies. The winkies were a quiet rather fearful race but they were under the command of the Witch so when she gave them sharp spears and told them to destroy them, the poor winkies didn't have a chance." a couple of females fainted in fear.

"This time it was the lion who took command, he saw them marching towards them, their eyes on the girl so he stepped closer and roared. His roar was so ferocious the poor winkies ran back to the Witch where she beat each and everyone for failing her once more then she sent them right back to work." he kept going, he was so into his tale.

"When she calmed down the rumors say she went to her cupboard where she kept a golden cap. The cap was golden with rubies and diamonds, whoever had the cap was in control of the winged monkeys. The only drawback was the cap had the ability to be used 3 times." a chorus of "ooooooh" vibrated off the buildings.

"The witch already used it 2 times but I guess trying to get the girl and her friends she felt it was worth it, the winged monkeys destroyed her friends or so they thought but they were unable to harm the girl due to the mark on her forehead where the good witch kissed her. After all, everyone knows good is stronger than evil so they took her to the witch to let her decide." he smiled when his audience cheered.

"The way she destroyed the witch was intense, she threw a bucket of water onto her and the witch melted," he concluded his story with a bow.

"If only I had known this years ago, I would have made sure I destroyed her then I could be famous and have everyone bowing down to me." I thought to myself.

I wonder why there were so many witches and wizards who take over the lands from hard workers and make them slaves. It made no sense to me but I never did understand how big people think if they think at all. I knew of the Witches even the wizard but most of the time I stayed away from them.

I came across the witch of the west just once, she was pretty horrific. The munchkins didn't have a chance. She wore all black which of course you know is common for witches to wear. She was a fearsome one, just to look at her would cause fear to settle in your chest.

She didn't enslave anyone when I first met her. It was purely by accident our paths crossed I was walking and thinking. Next thing I knew I felt fear creeping into my chest, it was as if a feeling suddenly became alive. My throat felt as if it was closing up, my heart began beating faster than it ever did before.'

"What are you doing here?" she screeched at me causing my blood to freeze in my veins.

"I-I" my voice stopped working as I saw others coming along the path behind her. I wanted to warn them but I was unable to say a word.

They didn't notice her at first when they did it was pandemonium, they yelled and tried to get out of her way. She laughed but it was more a cackle and began to chase them. It looked like a game of cat and mouse but much worse. When she caught a couple of the munchkins she said they would be mulch for the forest.

I'm not sure what she did with them but I had a feeling she was going to put them into one of the trees and just let them die there. The trees were alive and very angry if anyone other than the witch tried to enter they would be thrown by the branches. Even the smallest of munchkins were unable to enter the woods without fear of being injured or at the worst ripped apart. I had seen those trees ripping animals apart, each tree took a limb of the animal and ripped it was brutal but they seemed to thrive on the carnage.

I decided to get out of the line of fire, since there were so many running around, the witch shooting off smoke I took it as the perfect time to make my getaway. I felt bad not knowing if they made it out alive but when you are dealing with a witch it's everyone for themselves.

The first time I saw the wizard it was truly an amazing thing, he came floating across in a huge colorful piece of material filled with air. He was strong and I knew he was an amazing wizard. Those who saw him were in awe of his amazing powers. He built the emerald city with the help of the munchkins who wanted to build him a city fit to be ruled by him.

CHAPTER 4

So many stories I could tell but right now I am going to keep telling the one I started. You see since the witch was so evil, the fact she was gone caused many folks to think the girl and her entourage were more powerful than any creature whoever came to these lands.

They were shown to the rooms they had been in before, I know they expected to be sent for immediately because they had done as the wizard demanded so in their eyes they were the witch killers and if truth be told the girl killed two witches so she thought herself high and mighty. She kept insisting on returning to Kansas, I guess is the kingdom she ruled over.

It took days for the Wizard to send for them. I knew they were talking amongst themselves how they didn't deserve to be treated in such a manner. The scarecrow asked the girl in green to deliver a message to the wizard. If he did not grant them an audience he would call the winged monkeys. Since the witch was killed the cap now belonged to the girl so I guess her friends felt they had the right to decide how to use it.

I thought the wizard would tell them to go away but he sent for them right away or at least by 9 the next morning. When they entered the throne room they were terrified as they weren't sure what form he would take since the wizard could take any form at all he wanted.

The throne room was vast, it would fit the entire munchkin land in it and then some, it was dark when they first entered but the lanterns on the wall would light as they walked in which would cause shadows on the walls to see as if they were dancing.

They cowered together, the tin man was shaking so bad he sounded like tin cans being dragged over a street by a string. The scarecrow was too busy staring at the flames in the lantern which was understandable. The lion was sitting on the floor holding his tail, his face the perfect picture of fear.

The girl was scared but she was staring at the throne as if expecting the wizard to rise out of it and she was ready to bow before him. As she stood there a solemn voice boomed out over the room.

"I am Oz the great and terrible " it echoed off the walls and doubled so it sounded as if it was coming from everywhere all at once. "Why do you seek me?"

They were looking everywhere but were unable to find where the voice was coming from. "Where are you?" the girl asked fear causing her voice to tremble.

"I am everywhere," answered the Voice, "but to the eyes of common mortals, I am invisible. I will now seat myself upon my throne, that you may converse with me." Indeed, the Voice seemed just then to come straight from the throne itself; so they walked toward it and stood in a row while Dorothy said

"We have come to claim our promises" her voice seemed to get a little stronger with each word she said.

"What promises?" the voice demanded.

"You promised to send me home," the girl said which caused each of her group to demand what they wanted.

"You promised me a brain," the scarecrow said.

"You promised me a heart" the still quivering tinman declared.

"You promised me courage," the lion said as he held his tail like a child's blanket.

"Is she really dead?" the voice no longer sounded so strong. I saw the looks they exchanged, they were suspecting he wasn't what he seemed to be.

"Yes, I melted her with a bucket of water" the girl sounded defiant, I waited for the wizard to shoot fire at them for being impudent.

"Dear me" the voice became quiet, no longer booming off of the walls "I need some time to think. I will call for you when I am ready"

"You have had plenty of time to think " the tin man yelled.

"You have to keep your promises" the girl yelled, tears clogging her throat.

I guess the lion wanted to make the wizard afraid so he let out a roar that vibrated off the walls. The roar caused the small loud thing was so startled he jumped away from the lion. When he jumped he crashed into a screen sitting near the throne.

When the screen fell it revealed an old man, he seemed startled to see them and startled he was seen. They were stunned while I was happy, you see I have known all along he was nothing special. When he first got here yes, I was in awe of him as much as anyone else but throughout the years I have come to know what he truly was.

The tin man not really guessing what was going on ran at the old man, his ax raised I'm not sure what he was going to do if he reached him. "Who are you?" the tin man shouted.

"I am Oz the great and terrible" the little old man looked at the floor. "But don't strike me--please don't--and I'll do anything you want me to."

The group looked at him in shock, each of them had a different experience the first time they saw him so their confusion to find out he was just a simple man was rather upsetting.

"I thought you were a great head," the girl said as tears fell down her cheeks.

"I thought he was a lovely Lady," said the Scarecrow he scowled at the man.

"I thought he was a terrible Beast," said the Tinman still shaking some from the memory.

"I thought he was a Ball of Fire," exclaimed the Lion, as the scarecrow flinched at the thought.

"You are all wrong. I am none of those" he seemed sad but I wasn't falling for it. He was telling them about how the Emerald city was built. He finally admitted to someone how it truly wasn't so bright but the glasses he made everyone wear blinded them to the truth. He failed to tell them about how the workers were treated when they were helping to build the city.

He was a brutal taskmaster when he was younger, I thought he mellowed with age but he did tell a young girl and her misfit group to go kill a witch so it is possible he truly was still wicked.

You see he called the witches wicked but they were merely doing what they were born to do. The witches in the North and South could have been wicked but they needed to balance out the scales.

You know of course how there has to be a balance of good and evil for things to survive. If there is too much of one or the other the balance is not met.

Personally, the city was fine as it was. The glasses hid the true beauty of Emerald City, it wasn't because of it's opulence everyone loved it. It was because everyone got along,there was no arguing about what belonged to who it was simply home. He claims he was the one who built the city but I was the one who planned out where every stone would go he simply came along and took over.

He confessed to them he was nothing but they still wanted him to do as he promised which made sense but I could see the tinman had a heart. The lion was as courageous as any feline then came the scarecrow he was smarter than he gave himself credit for.

The so called wizard could only supply them with tangible evidence of something they already possessed. It was rather confusing but then I saw the girl standing off to the side looking sad, I knew when I was younger I could have helped but I was quite older now so I had to do what I could to help the so called wizard.

"Come now, you know what to do" I made my presence known.

He looked at me and said "I will think of what I can do, Please make yourselves comfortable and come see me in a couple days"

After they left I told him we could build a balloon and he would be able to take her home but in his absence he was to have the scarecrow rule over them because he would be a perfect match.

It took a couple days but soon he was ready to go with the help of Dorothy and her friends. They were more than willing to go above and beyond for her since she was the one who supported and helped them.

The day of the big launch, something happened I was not expecting. Toto, I still think he was a small loud thing, had run off after another small creature and Dorothy was trying to get him. The balloon was pulling at the ropes, as she got close enough to the basket the ropes cracked and the balloon flew off into the air.

"Oh my" Dorothy was crushed. Her friends received what they wanted but she was left behind.

"Miss Dorothy" I told her even though her friends got their hearts desires and she missed out of hers there was a way for her to get what she wanted. She had already tried the winged monkeys who told her there was no way, I told her if she and her friends travel to the South they could ask Glinda if she could help.

I wish I knew what happened to her next, when they left I stayed behind to help the Emerald City transition for when the scarecrow came back. I only hope her and the yappy one found their way home.

THE END

KIM PLASKET

Kim Plasket is a Jersey girl at heart relocated to sunny Florida. She enjoys writing mainly horror and paranormal stories and lives with her husband and two kids. When she is not slaving away at her day job, she can be found drinking coffee with fellow author Valerie Willis and planning the demise of some poor character. Currently, she has several short stories featured in anthologies such as 'Demonic Wildlife' and 'The Hunted', also has a story in an Anthology Titled Fireflies and Fairy dust she also has had a story featured in Shades of Santa. Also the newly released DrabbleDark Anthology, Work of hearts magazine. She has stories in Trembling With Fear, more tales from the tree, Thrill of the Hunt: Buried Alive, and Demonic Carnival: First Ticket's free. She also has several short stories and a post for Women in Horror Month on the website The Horror Tree.

https://www.amazon.com/-/e/B074YCLRCF

https://twitter.com/KimPlasket

HUCK AND THE MOMO
HUCKLEBERRY FINN

Josh Pritchett

I had been living with the Widow Douglas and her sister Miss Watson for the better part of a year when Pap found me. He'd found out about that six thousand dollars I'd gotten after me and Tom Sawyer had found Injun Joe's hidden treasure and Pap wanted it for hisself. After he'd gone a round or two in the courts with the Widow and Judge Thatcher over who'd been rearing me, Pap took me on a raft three miles up the Mississippi to a cabin in the Illinois woods.

We'd hunt and fish and smoke and cuss up a storm. I and didn't mind not having no lessons or doing all that praying the Widow made me do. But I didn't care much none for the cowhiding Pap gave me every day.

When he'd get a few in him, Pap would rail on about the government and freed slaves being allowed to dress fancy. He'd get so fired that he'd clap me hard on the back of the neck some.

But the worse part was him tying me up and leaving me in that cabin alone while he went to take some of the stuff we hunted and fished to town to get himself some jugs of corn liquor. He'd let me go and start to drink that liquor while I'd have to make him dinner.

One time he starts cowhiding me again till I was blue and bloody and then he stumbled to his sleeping rags mumbling something. I lay there on that dirt floor feeling pain and madness coming over me and I decided that maybe I could be damned, but I'd make sure my Pap got here first!

By the light of his candle, I got me that gun down and cocked it. I was gonna point it at his head when I heard something from outside. Something heavy that crunched down the bushes and sticks and then came a smell that was just like rotten eggs and underarm sweat.

I about choked on that stink and then Pap woke up and looked around and saw me with the gun. "What you doing with that," he says looking scared.

Huck and The Momo by Josh Pritchett

It made me happy to see him scared like that. I could of ended him then and there, but then I realized that I'd done lost my nerve.

"I heard something," I says. "Some'n outside the cabin!"

He blinked and wanted to know why I didn't rouse him. I says I was gonna lie and wait.

Then we hear it, someone beaten on the side of a tree with a big stick. Just going 'tok, tok, tok,' like on a big drum. "Damn them," he slurs as he gets to his feet and grabbed the gun away from me.

"Damn y'all," he shouted as he pulled the door open and stumbled out.

Pap pointed his gun to the woods and fired off a barrel. The sound echoed through the woods and stirred up all kinds of critters we could hear. "Git off my land," he yelled.

The moon was pretty full that night and we could see real good. Good enough to see a rock come flying out the woods and hitting the cabin wall close to where Pap was standing with his gun and making this loud 'Crack' noise.

"Lard'," he cursed and nearly ran me over as he got back into the cabin.

We held up and there till sun up. We didn't see what it was that threw the rock at Pap, though we thought we might half hear something moving round outsides. Pap finally decided we should go hunting and catch us some breakfast.

We were wandering around looking for some game, but them woods was empty except for us. "Why' it so quiet?" Pap muttered as he held the gun.

The sun's yellow light was coming in through the trees, making all the trees look dark and shadowy. I was looking around, wondering if I could give Pap the slip and runaways before he could catch me.

I didn't smell that stink till Pap fired off a round at the trees and I look to see what he shot. But I only saw something big and hairy rush off into the trees.

"Did you see it!" Pap said. "It run off before I could draw a bead."

"A bear?" I says and he clapped me hard enough to knock me down to the ground.

"No, ijit," he says. "This weren't no bear. It stood on two legs, it did, and it had a big ol' round head like a melon, stood up."

I look up at him and thought real fast, like Tom Sawyer did. "A Momo," I says.

"A what?"

Mind you, I didn't believe he done seen anything but a bear. But I thought, maybe this could get me aways from Pap once and for all. "A Momo," I says. "Is a giant ape from Africa. Some folks brought a couple over to sell to a zoo in New York City. But them big monkeys got away and started living up here and the woods before breeding and making more Momos. I read about them in school!"

Pap hadn't liked me going to school none. When he found out I could read and write, he was mad enough that he almost went after the Widow Douglas for sending me to school. But now as I made up this lie about the Momo, Pap was right interested. So, I tried to lay it on thick as butter.

"There was this one feller who caught one and sold it to the zoo in New York City for a million dollars."

"A million dollars," Pap says as his eyes lit up like a firecracker.

Pap's eyes moved back and forth as he tried to plan and scheme how he was gonna catch that Momo. We went back to the cabin and to my surprise, Pap didn't touch any that corn whiskey. He was trying to be clear-headed for once as he reckon on how he was gonna catch that Momo.

I'd dozed off some while Pap was at his scheming when he roused me up again. "Come on," he says. "We're gonna dig us a pit!"

We spent that day and most of the next digging us a deep hole in the ground in a clearing just inside the tree line. Pap had a ladder to get us in and out of the pit as it got deeper. According to his calculations, that there Momo was well over six feet if it was an inch!

That night Pap didn't bother to tie me up. He must have known I was too tired after all that digging to run off from him.

When we got that pit done, Pap had me saw some tree limbs to cover it over and I'd seen the old man so proud of himself when it was finished. "Now," he says. "We gotta bait it."

Then he looks at me and he says to me. "Say, what that book say about them Momos like to eat?"

Thinking quick, I reckoned that the Momo, which I still thought was a bear, would probably like to eat fish and berries. So, Pap and I went and fished up some trout ten picked some wild berries not too far from the cabin. Then we laid them out good on the branches Pap was using to cover the hole. If 'in a Momo or bear come along and smelt that feast, it'd be in the trap for sure.

"What else, Boy?" Pap demanded. "What else does it like?"

I decided maybe I'd try and push my luck a bit and I told him that the Momo females rut around with skunks to attract the males. "It's like French perfume to 'um," I says.

Well, Pap's eyes went wide at that news. "O' all the damned things," he said and spat a wad of tobacco on the ground.

"That's was the book says," I says.

Pap grumbled and then he went looking for a skunk. Well, he found himself one and I swear I didn't know that skunks could run that fast or that Pap could either!

That skunk took off when it saw Pap acoming and it ran back and forth like while Pap chased it through the bushes 'acussing at it. Every time Pap got close, that skunk would squirt on him until Pap smelled worse than that skunk or the Momo Bear. I tried not to laugh none so as not to risk a cowhiding.

I think Pap thought to squirt that skunk on me and offer me up to the Momo as a bride. But in the end, Pap would have to serve as the bride of the Momo.

Well, that was settled, and we proceeded to hunker down and wait on our Momo. Night came and we was still out there waiting. Pap had stayed sober the whole day and if I didn't dislike him so much, I might of been kinda proud of him.

He held onto to that gun in case he'd half to wound it som. We had us a lantern, but we weren't gonna turn it on unless something fell into our trap. My plan for how I was gonna get out of there was mostly, I reckon, on luck.

I figured that Pap's Momo would wander over to the bait and fall into that pit. Then after that, Pap would be awfully proud of hisself and begin drinking to celebrate what he'd done. When he got all passed out, I'd pretend that the Momo had gotten lose and killed me by leaving a bloody shirt and then let out for the river. I'd get myself away from there and never look back none.

All this relied on luck. But I was getting desperate and just wanted to get away from Pap before he killed me.

The moon rose above us and give us some light to see, but not real well. Pap took out a pouch of chewing tobacco and got himself a pinch before handing it to me. I took one and went to hand it back to him, but he told me to keep it and I stuffed it in my pocket.

Then I smelled something worse than Pap coming from the woods!

It was that same stink from before, rotten eggs mixed with underarm sweat. Pap must of smelled it too cause he tensed up some and held that gun tight. I didn't see it too well, but I heard it coming out of the woods as it popped branches and leaves under its feet. I could hardly see Pap then either, just make them out like.

Then I heard this sniffing sound like hound dogs make when they've gotta scent and then it made a kinda "OOK, OOK, OOK," sound. I reckon then, do bears make a noise like that?

I could feel my heart speed up a I heard that sniffing sound get closer to our trap. Then it made another 'OOK," sound, it sounded more curious and happy, like it though it was getting a treat or some kind.

Then me and Pap heard something heavy go crashing into the pit and there was dis loud howl that sounded like whatever it was 's scared almost to death.

"We dun it," Papa shouts and hops up still holding his gun.

I turned on the lantern and followed him, thinking I'd only see a bear. But what I saw I'll never forget.

When I shown the light into the pit, dis thing looks back at us and is just howling and crying and I know it ain't no bear. This thing had arms and hands like a man, but longer and bigger. It was all covered in the blackest hair you ever did see like it was covered in black charcoal ash. But the face was what bothered me cause it looked almost human.

Pap was dancing around shouting. "A million dollars, a million dollars!" Over and over.

Then we heard it, a roar unlike anything either of us had heard before. It was so loud, that I thought it shook the trees around us. Then we heard 'um come crashing out of the woods.

"Lordy," I heard Pap say before we let out back towards the cabin!

We could hear them coming and jumping towards us as that youngin' (I later reckon' that what it was) howled and carried on. Then as we ran, them things was throwing rocks at us. One of them made this whizzing sound as it flew pass my ear, it was that close.

I'm not rightly sure how we made it back to the cabin, but when we did, Pap and me blocked the door. Then for a minute or so, it got all quiet. "Listing," Pap says still holding the gun. Then the whole cabin shook as something hit the side of the cabin hard enough to buckle the wooden slates.

That was when a big rock, about half the size of a bag of feed, smashed the window and crashed against the wall on the other side.

Huck and The Momo by Josh Pritchett

"LORDY!" Pap screamed when he saw it.

Something hit the side of the cabin again and that time I heard the wooden walls crack!

I guess Pap finally remembered he had a gun with him and he tried to take a shot. I don't know if me was scared just couldn't see nothing and the dark. Then one of them rocks hit the lantern and we had us a fire. "LORDY, LORDY!" Pap called out, but I weren't waiting for the lord,

Instead, I hauled myself out of there through one of them holes those rocks had made and tried to make my way to the river when one of them came out from behind some trees and looked at me. I could just make it out in the light coming from the fire. Its nose was flattened and the mouth and chin was set like it was on half a ball. The place where the eyebrows ought of been were just sticking out over the eyes like a hat brim. But them eyes was what I found most stupefying. I guess I'd say they looked human!

Then I notice that it was holding the little one we caught in the trap and I thought "Well, I'm dead for sure now!"

The little one made this 'Whoop' sound and the Mama Momo look at me then she grabbed a hold of me and picked me up liken I weighed nothing at all and went to take me off into the trees. I struggle to get loose from the mama, but it was no use. She had a hold of me and I was along for the ride.

I reckon them Momos was gonna eat me. But instead, she took me and her youngin' up to some caves see back in the woods real deep. When we got there I saw did big old Momo who was as tall as the side of the Widow Douglas' house with arms as big around as trees that come down almost to his knees.

By then the sun was coming up and could make out from the look on its face that he weren't too happy that mama had brought me there.

He looked at me and give me this growl and the mama she hissed at him. I reckon he was the king of the Momos cause all them others sort of deferred to him and moved back while he and the mama hashed it out.

He'd grunt and bark at her and she'd go to hissing and making these "Ot, ot, ot," sounds.

Finally, the king made one more bark before turning and walking off and knew then I was adopted by the Mama Momo!

I wondered then if the Widow Douglas knew she had herself a soul mate out amongst the Momo and what she'd think if ins she knew that.

Well, the next couple of days weren't too bad. That little Momo liked to razzle me some and he'd laugh while he was doing so I knew he didn't mean no harm by it. Sometimes Mama Momo would have to break things up if she thought we was getting too rough for her liking.

All and all they then treat them too bad. I liked the young Momo and Mama Momo, but King Momo kept giving me the eye whenever he saw me. Can't say I blame him none. But they fed me, though I can't say I cared for raw fish too much, these folks didn't know nothing about fire.

But after a couple of days, I thought I might want to get out of there. Not because they was mean to me, they treated me better than Pap ever did. But I was used to being on my own and I then want Mama Momo to make me into a Momo anymore then I wanted the Widow Douglas to make me civilized.

I tried to think on a plan to get myself out of there. Me and the Momos were sitting in this grove of trees. The Momos were just resting and taking some shade while I sat dipping some chew a little bit aways from them. 'Bout then the King Momo spies me and what I'm doing. Then he comes over to look at me and my dipping and I just look back at him. By then I reckon' on what he's so curious about and I hold out the pouch to him.

The King Momo took it in his thumb and trigger finger and looked at it. Then he sniffed it and let out a low growl. I sat there looking at him still chewing my pinch when he reaches in and takes a big wad of it. I was a bit annoyed since that was likely the last bit of chewing tobacco I was gonna come across for a while, but the saw the King Momo swallow it!

This awful look comes over the King Momo's face like he knows something is very wrong and I just hope he ain't gonna throw up on me. Just then he turns his head and grabs his neck like it's on fire and just lets out a bellow that sounded like a braying mule.

All the other Momos turn to see what was happening and run over to King Momo as he's grabbing he's neck like it was on fire. Well, I watch for a couple of seconds and when I see that their all paying attention to him, I get to my feet and I high tailed it out of there.

I ran just fast as I could. As I did, I could hear the Momos howling out through the woods. I guess somes of them took off after me, but I didn't look back. Instead I poured on the speed until I found my way back to the river and found Pap's raft that he used to haul me there.

Then out of them woods come the Kid Momo. At first I thought he was gonna grab me at take me back to the King Momo. But then he starts pointing at the raft and gesturing back n' forth between us and I understood that the Kid Momo wanted to go with me.

"Well, hop on," I says and we headed on down the river.

We heard one last big roar from the Momos as the raft sailed out to the middle of the river and drifted down the old river.

The Kid Momo couldn't speak none, so I had to sus out why it was he wanted to come with me. I thought maybe his Pap was like my Pap, just mean and bad. Or maybe Kid Momo didn't have no other friends other than me.

Of course I knew it was gonna be mighty strange when people come along on the river and sees me with this Momo, but then I had a spot of luck and found a big piece of canvas that I used to make a wigwam for Kid Momo to lie in during the day so no one would sees him.

One night, we sailed up to a small island in the middle of the river and noticed a campfire. I sailed up to it and landed the raft before mossing up to the fire. I saw it was Miss Watson's slave Jim.

Jim about threw a fit when he saw me and the Kid Momo come up to his fire. But after I convinced Jim I was no ghost come to haunt him and the Kid Momo was okay too, Jim relaxed and told me that everyone in town thought Pap had killed me, but they couldn't put him in jail cause they ain't found my body. Then he tells me that Pap's been telling everyone how I was taken by these giant monkeys and he'll give any man a share of his million dollars if they'll go with him to find them giant monkeys.

Jim looked at Kid Momo. "I reckon that part is true."

Then I told Jim about living with the Momos and how me and Kid Momo was letting out on our own. Jim asked if he could come along till he could find a way to buy his family's freedom and I reckon he could.

So the three of us sailed on down the river together. Jim and Kid Momo had to stay in the wigwam most days in case of bounty hunters. Me and Jim got used to Kid Momo's smell and we got him used to eaten' cooked fish which he seemed to like.

Kid Momo, Jim and me we had us a heck of a time after that. We sailed on down the river and eventually I taught Kid Momo how to steer and paddle the raft. Which came in handy if we got stuck on a sandbar or a muddy bottom cause Kid Momo was so strong, didn't have no trouble getting us out of it.

Then we met up with a couple of fellers who been run out of some town. They called themselves named the Duke and the King, but they weren't real royalty. They were just a couple of liars was all but I didn't want to make a big deal out of it.

They both about fell off the raft when they saw Kid Momo come out of the wigwam. But after they calmed down, the King says. "Why, that there beast could be the key to our restorations!"

The King told us that we could show Kid Momo to folks and charge them money for it. I wasn't too keen on it, but then the Duke told me there'd be no harm in it. So we stopped in this one town where everyone had gone to a revival and the Duke snuck into the print shop and made up some bills that read.

Come one and all to see the eighth wonder of the world. The Magnificent Momo! Is it man or is it ape? You be the judge! Ten cents for adults, five cents for children!

Well, that was interesting and me and Jim using some finger pointing and signals we worked out with Kid Momo told him what we wanted to do and he seemed to understand what we wanted to do and agreed.

Next the King went out to that revival and announced to one and all that there would be a show the next night. "We've found us the master of the woods, Ladies and Gentlemen," he said. "A modern spectacle of the ages. The Magnificent Momo, the American Ape Man!"

The next night, The King had found hisself some fancy clothes and then introduced hisself as Dr. Armstrong, an expert on the North American Ape. He went and spun some yarn about how he found Kid Momo out in the woods and done brung him back to civilization so everyone could see the wonder of the North American Ape Man.

The Duke would sit in the audience and declare that the Kid Momo was just somebody in a monkey costume, but then the King as Dr. Armstrong would demonstrate that it weren't by having Kid Momo lift a big rock me and Jim would find. For good measure, he arranged to have the show in the townhall.

I was having second thoughts about all this before Jim reminded me that we needed some money if we was gonna keep on down the river and he still wanted to buy his family's freedom. I had to say he made some fine arguments. But still felt wrong about it.

Jim and me found a good-sized rock down by the river and brought it back in a wheelbarrow we borrowed. It would have been easier if Kid Momo would have carried it for us, but the King reasoned that Kid Momo should stay out of sight till showtime. Once there Jim and me worked it onto the stage as the King and the Duke worked out their lines for that night.

Me and Jim set up the candles on the stage and then I went to collect the money out front. When the show started, the King stepped out onto the stage. "Ladies and gentlemen," he said talking with an English accent. "Tonight, I present to you, the wonder of the ages. The eighth wonder of the world! The Momo, the North America Ape Man!"

'N at that point, Jim led Kid Momo out onto the stage. I watched and thought this didn't feel right and I could tell Jim was feeling the same way. Kid Momo was smiling and looking around as folks were "Oooing," and "Awwing" him. A few even covered their nose's on account of the smell coming from Kid Momo.

"Shouldn't that be in a cage?" One fella' called out.

"No, no friends, I assure you that the Momo is a most docile creature as you've ever seen."

Then the Duke yelled out. "That ain't nothing but someone in a monkey costume!"

The crowd starts murmuring and talking low. But then the King says. "Ah, but you're wrong, Friend."

The King pointed to the rock and says. "I call on any man here to lift this here rock!"

A few men came up and gave it a go, but couldn't hardly lift it none without help. Finally, the King tells everyone that the Momo will lift it. Jim pointed to the rock and made like to show Kid Momo what to do. Kid Momo made a grunt and nodded his understanding.

Then Kid Momo squatted down and took and picked up that rock up over his head like it was nothing. The crowd started cheering and clapping their hands. "Say, where'd you find him?" One fellow called out. "I bet he'd be worth more than ten of my negroes."

My blood set to boil when I heard that, and I could see that Jim knew this was wrong too. "Well, folks," the King says in his English accent. "I had plans to take this Momo around the world to show him off, but I might be persuaded to auction him off for the right price!"

Well, that was it as far as I was concerned. I caught Kid Momo's eye as he was still holding that rock and I gestured that he should throw it. Kid Momo hauled off and tossed that big rock as hard as he could at the wall and some of the women screamed and the men just looked around.

Jim caught on to my meaning and he gestured that Kid Momo should toss the King next, which he did right at the Duke before all them people jumped out of their seats and made a dash for the door. I pounded my chest like I'd seen the King Momo do and Kid Momo did the same as people ran for it thinking that the Mom had gone rabid or something.

After that the three of us let out of there real quick, leaving the King and the Duke and got ourselves back to the raft before the townsfolk could catch us. But the kept the money we'd made from the take.

We sailed for a day or so before Kid Momo went to smelling something. Before I could reckon' what was going on, he jumped off the raft and headed for the shore. Jim and me tried to go after him to find out what was going on, but he had left us behind.

Eventually, Jim and me found out through Tom Sawyer that Miss Watson had passed and freed Jim in her will. He used the money from the take to buy his family's freedom. I learned form Judge Thatcher that Pap had drunk himself to death and told everyone I'd been stolen away by these giant monkeys. When he asked if there was any truth to that, I told the Judge that it was just the rambling of an old drunk.

I saw my friend one more time after that as I was sailing up that river, the captain of my own steamboat. I was looking out at the spot where I had last seen him and he just stepped on out of the trees like he knew I was there. He'd gotten as big as old King Momo and I saw he had a couple of youngin's with him and I knew what had happened.

I waved back at my old friend as my boat headed on up the Mississippi.

LIPS AS RED AS BLOOD
SNOW WHITE

Jamie Zaccaria

I always knew there was something wrong with my stepmother and what she did in the lowest level of our castle; I could hear the screams at night. They came from the basement but were so loud that their residue lingered in my bedroom two floors up. When my father married her, she was beautiful like an ice statue. She never ate, she never danced and she never laughed. She was a pristine sculpture whose interest was only peaked by the reflection she spotted when walking by a mirror.

Then my father died and everything changed. She turned from ice to fire...burning up everything and everyone in her path. She chased away his closest advisors and replaced them with somber-faced men from foreign countries who rarely spoke. A darkness soon spread over the entire kingdom, not just the feeling of despair but eventually a tangible pattern of death. Each year the crop yield was less, the children more sickly and even the sun seemed further away.

She seemed to hate happiness, banning the dinners and balls that my father used to love. What she hated most of all though, was me. The older I got, the more enraged she became at merely seeing me in the room. Whereas I used to sleep in the West Wing near the King's quarters, I was quickly moved down to the floor below me; demoted to a position physically and socially lower than bequeathed to me by my heredity. My handmaidens were removed and I was no longer given an allowance to buy new clothing. Eventually I was no longer treated as royalty at all. I was only another young girl scuttling through the corners seeking to avoid the Queen's wrath.

As I got older, people started to notice me again. They whispered about how beautiful I was and how much I looked like my mother. Hearing this only enraged my stepmother more. That was when I was forced into a room in the basement where the screams were so loud that they drowned out even the harshest of storms. I became a servant in my own home. But it kept me safe; away from her ice-cold eyes and away from whatever she did to make those people in the basement scream so loudly.

It was a dark, cold night when my curiosity got the best of me. Or perhaps it was my fear. Either way, I made the disastrous decision of following those screams. I just couldn't take it anymore; all night the sounds of torture and pain. So I got up and went to the door at the end of the hall. Without thinking, I pushed it open. My eyes followed the sounds of agony that my ears had already been stalking.

That's when I saw my beautiful stepmother hovering over a table dripping wet. The room resembled a dungeon with chains hanging from the ceiling and strange-looking metal contraptions hiding in dark corners. When my eyes got used to the darkness I realized she wasn't just wet- she was covered in blood. The scarlet substance was everywhere: the table, the floor, all over her clothes and hands. But worse than that was what was tightly gripped in her hands: a pulsating and dripping mass.

My eyes darted to the right and I gasped when I saw the half-naked man chained to the wall. He had a giant black gaping hole in his chest underneath where his ribcage should have been sealed together. That's when I realized that the organ my stepmother was holding was his heart. She had cut his heart out.

Then she did the most appalling and frightening thing I have ever seen. She bent her head to the organ in her hands and I realized suddenly why I had never seen her eat food before. My stepmother ate hearts. I made a choked sound at this disturbing and sudden insight, and she heard me, snapping her head almost inhumanly in my direction. Her lips dripped with blood that not a moment ago pumped through the fleshy bulb in her hands.

I cried out when I noticed her face. My stepmother's beautiful icy visage had transformed into a monstrous vision that I had only seen in my childhood nightmares. Her eyes shone a bright golden color and her teeth gleamed sharply. They were covered in blood. She made a hissing sound and that's when I finally snapped out of my stupor.

I ran away from the door and through the dark hallways of the castle. I knew that I had to get as far away from my stepmother as possible. I ran and ran until I had left the castle and its grounds behind. I was only in my nightgown and the cold bit at my skin, yet I never slowed my pace. I ran until I reached the edge of the woods. I had always feared this place but now thought nothing of continuing forward.

There was snow on the ground and the stark white color of it contrasted sharply with the black twisted forms of tree branches, but even the dark unknown was less frightening to me than what I was running away from. I'm not sure how long I ran through the frigid, dark forest. I just knew that I could never go back. I knew that the next time I saw her would be the death of me.

At some point during my race I came upon a clearing. There was a small stone cottage surrounded by a tall angry looking gate. I slowed down and tried to catch my breath. I could hear dead tree branches knocking up against rotted wooden shutters. The sounds of owls mixed with the howling of the wind. It was so cold that my lips and fingers had turned numb and the snow had soaked right through my slippers. I knew that if I stayed out in the forest all night I would surely die, so I decided to take my chances with the house.

Walking through the creaky front gate I approached the front door. I took a deep breath and summoned the last of my courage. After knocking on the door three times I realized that no one was home. I also realized that the door was unlocked. In any normal circumstances, I would never have entered a strange structure in the middle of the woods. But I was freezing and exhausted and had just about given up hope. It seemed that this abode was my last savior.

Inside the cottage was dark. I could tell that it was not deserted, as it was filled with homely delights. Dirty mugs littered the tabletop and articles of clothing were haphazardly thrown about. I shut the door behind me and took a few steps inside. There was a menagerie of weapons lining the walls. Axes, swords, bow and arrows, wooden stakes, and more covered the room in a sort of morbid wallpaper. I shivered to myself.

Walking over to the fireplace I noticed what seemed like a recent pile of soot. Shaking with cold, I removed a log from the pile in the corner of the room and put it in the fireplace, using the accompanying piece of flint to light the barest of flames. I carefully caressed the air around the flickering orange light until it became strong enough to survive on its own and provide me the warmth I so desperately needed. As the heat from the fire slowly soaked into my chilled body I became tired. I lay down on the woven rug, pulling a nearby blanket on top of me. Within moments I was fast asleep.

I awoke to a thundering noise as many sets of heavy footsteps descended into the cottage. They noticed me before my vision cleared enough for me to decipher who they were. Dwarves. There were seven of them. Each had a long beard of varying colors. Each was covered in dirt and grime. I noticed that the sun had recently risen, its rays shooting through the open doorway behind them, making these small figures look almost angelic.

Somehow they knew who I was before I could formally introduce myself. They had been foretold of my coming, or else were not surprised to see me. Suffice it to say, they were more than hospitable, especially when they learned who I was running from. These dwarves were not just miners, although their excavation of precious gems did provide them a living. It turned out they were also Watchers. Their kind had been dedicated sentinels of the forest and the creatures within it.

They were more than familiar with my stepmother the Queen. The leader of the group, the tallest and strongest of the dwarves with a salt and pepper beard, explained it to me.

"Ever since she married your father a darkness had been creeping into the forest," his deep voice said. "Slowly but surely her evil has been infecting the spirits of the woods and servants continue to go missing from the nearby villages."

I was warned that it was my sacred duty to kill my stepmother and restore my kingdom. This I was desperately terrified of. I protested, telling them what I saw the night I ran away. How could I, a slight and mortal girl, defeat such a demon? They would teach me.

From the first dwarf, the leader, I learned about a world I had never even dreamed of. This is the world where my stepmother came from and its evil is that which threatened to strangle the last bit of life from my kingdom. He showed me old books, volumes of leather-bound yellow pages that explained and elaborated upon this darkness.

Once I had the knowledge, I needed to learn how to defeat this demoness who had usurped me. Three of the dwarves were experts in weaponry. I learned how to use a sword, a bow and arrow, and an ax. I strengthened my muscles and my mind so that I could wield these instruments of death without shaking and without uncertainty.

The fifth dwarf was quiet and reserved. He brought me into the forest and taught me the hidden souls of living things. He showed me how to recognize the rot that was encroaching upon the ecosystem. He instructed me in survival as well- which berries were safe to eat and how to avoid poisonous plants. From him I learned not to fear the forest but instead to worship it.

I was retaught my heritage by the sixth dwarf. He reminded me of who I was and where I came from. He knew everything about my father and the fathers that came before him. He re-instilled in me the deepest honor for my bloodline- one I had lost in the years of servitude to the villain who now ruled where I should.

The last dwarf was the most mysterious. He had a twinkle in his eye as he bade me follow him. Quick as a sparrow, he flitted about the cottage, grabbing herbs and other ingredients that all went into the large iron kettle warming over the fire. He tinkered with it for three days until finally it released a bright green steam. Then he gathered the others and pulled out a shiny silver blade.

This concoction was supposed to be my key to defeating my heart-eating stepmother. It would imbue me with the strength, stealth, wisdom, and power needed to make my mortal self a worthy opponent. I was to consume the potion and then use the silver blade to cut her heart out. Thanks to my training, I was no longer afraid of the woods or anything else that may get in my way and try to stop me.

The leader nodded his head and the others came to gather around the fire. One by one the dwarves stepped up to the kettle. Using the knife, each of them sliced their palm, letting their own blood become ingredients in the mysterious brew.

When it was ready, I dipped a copper mug into the kettle, pulling it out near full with the dark red liquid. It was thick and warm and contained unidentifiable chunks as it slid down my throat but I did not wince. I turned to the group, my lips a bright red from the blood that now stained them, and spoke.

"It's time."

Jamie Zaccaria

Jamie Zaccaria is a wildlife biologist by trade and writer by pleasure. She currently works for a wildlife conservation organization and writes fiction in her spare time. She is also a part-time Staff Writer for The Rational Online. She currently lives in New Jersey with her girlfriend, cats and pit-bull. For a complete portfolio, please visit www.jamiezaccaria.com.

www.jamiezaccaria.com

twitter.com/JamieRoseGold1

THE WINE-DARK SEA
THE ODYSSEY

Larry Griffin

The wine-dark sea, raging and wrathful, rolled under the obsidian skies. Odysseus stood there at the bow of his ship and looked at the waves. He had always been told he could own the world. But he had to admit, the recent events had been challenging that. It had been exhilarating at first, all the battles. But he was tired now. His bed, with his wife there, seemed more appealing by the day, though he could not tell his men this. They'd just think him a coward and a pansy.

The men were all annoyed and hungry, their stomachs rumbling. They'd been fed so fat on the island with Circe, but that was a day and a half behind them now, and the ocean and their stomachs seemed to both roll in unison.

"Listen, men," he said, trying to sound authoritative and commanding – it was the exhausting task, always trying to be this way, never having the time to stop. "We're going to pass by the land of the sirens, who'll try and enchant us with their song. They want to lure us to death on the rocks. They have no other purpose in life. But I have a plan for that..."

By the morning, they had tied his arms and his legs and he sat there like a cripple on the bow. The men rowed, but they'd be like silent sentries – there were globs of wax in all their ears. They'd passed through the storm-clouds and now the sky was a bright blue and the sea wafted a salty aroma over the waves that greeted them like a morning 'hello.'

Then they were coming upon the island. It was lush and green, adorned with bright flowers of all colors, a rainbow of them, and the whitest sand any of them had ever seen. And then came the rocks, where the sirens sat. They had the shape of women, but they were different somehow;

he couldn't have said how. They were slender and shapely but there was something in the eyes, he thought. He couldn't have told anyone exactly what it was. They were almost nude, save for bikini tops and grass skirts. Their hair, so blonde it was almost white, whipped wildly in the winds. It must have been uncomfortable, Odysseus thought briefly, for them to sit on those rocks.

But then that thought left him as they began to sing.

And their voices carried across the wind and waves – beautiful and melodious, although he couldn't have said what they were singing. They crooned and wailed and were making gestures with their hands. Come here, the hands seemed to say. Beckoning to the sirens' bodies, which, the more Odysseus looked, were anatomically flawless. There was not an inch of fat too much, and their proportions looked to be as absolutely symmetrical as they could be. It was like they were statues, only chiseled from living, delicate matter, the softest in the whole of creation.

They kept singing and beckoning, doing their dance on the rocks as the waves lapped like thirsty tongues against the stone. Odysseus felt something strange welling in him. It had been so damn long, after all, since he had been with a woman.

Struggling against the ropes, he cried out, "Wait for me! I'll get there eventually!"

His men rowed on. Now he had to crane his neck to see them. "I'll come back for you! What are your names? Goddamn, let me go! I'll swim there if I have to?" Their lithe forms were fading into the distance behind them now. Ahead, there was nothing even close to comparable in beauty.

But the sirens were unfazed. They kept dancing their dance, flowing in the wind, their skin caressed by sea-salt and licks of ocean tide.

———— ⌒⌒ ————

On the island, the three sirens finished their dance. The ship was gone, sailing off into the horizon. And they slowed their dance and began the short swim back to the island shore.

Most times, no one bothered them. They were an artist colony, and spent their time making baskets, planting food and, when the weather was nice, dancing on the rocks, honing their skills, feeling the sun on their skin and enjoying the stretching of muscles.

The issue was the men, delirious and half-crazy, who crashed their ships upon the rocks nearby when they saw the sirens dancing. It was a tragic thing and the sirens would hold fire-light vigils in the night for them, as the ships burned and the bodies decomposed and sank back into the ocean's limitless bounds.

The sirens were continually perplexed as to their effect on people. Of course they knew what they looked like. But what mandated the loss of control? Was physical beauty such an all-consuming thing? It wasn't as if anyone had ever tried to get to know them personally.

They discussed this as they made their way back to the island. It was of no matter to them. They would continue to display their art. It was the truest expression of themselves.

~

They were past the sirens and then on through the sea. The sky was clear blue but there were clouds on the far horizon, looming like bullies. Odysseus thought it was so strange to be out here with no cover. He could see everything on the Earth, he felt like. There was no mystery out here. And someday it seemed to him that the mystery would truly be gone, because the sea would be discovered. The world was finite. He needed there to be something unseen. It was the poetry that filled his soul, and without it, what would the world be?

They were coming now to the rock. It was white and sapphire, jutting toward the sky and shining brightly enough to force them all to look away. Odysseus felt the dread in him like a parasite, leeching at him. He'd not told any of the men what lay beyond there, because if they knew, they'd all piss their pants and cower and want to head back the way they'd come.

~

He donned his suit of armor, all gold and crimson. He had treasured this suit as a trophy. But in practice, it was hot, and he could feel sweat under his armpits. He'd stink by the time this was over.

The men were eyeing him. One of them, skinny and with a bearded stubble coating his chin, said, "Hey, the hell are you doing?"

He looked down and realized he had not come up with a convenient excuse. He said, "Just thought I'd try it on."

The blue rock stretched up at least 20 feet, casting them all in shadow.

It was a shade of color that none of them had ever seen — there was no natural blue in the world that was quite this bright, quite this intense. A cloud of white fog-mist enshrouded it at the top.

"You sure?" another man asked. This man was younger, baby-faced, and still had the last traces of acne pocking his upper cheeks. Odysseus remembered him as a hesitant boy, afraid to step on cockroaches or beetles. When they'd gone to battle, this boy's mother had taken Odysseus aside and told him that the boy needed to be protected, that he was strong but had too good of a heart to fight. Odysseus had told her that he'd do his best. Privately, he thought so what, the rest of us are cooked liver?

"Don't worry," Odysseus said, putting on his most confident possible front. Suddenly, for a brief moment, the lives of these men — boys, really — became very real to him and he had a sliver of doubt that began to uncoil in his gut like a snake. But he pushed it down. What were they to do? Go back? Sit there in the sea, immobile? He'd be a laughingstock. No, he thought, they had to press on.

A high mewling sound, like that of a puppy, filled the air. The sound was louder than any puppy Odysseus had ever encountered, though, ringing off the rock and the other rocks around them.

"The hell is that?" one man said — this man, Odysseus knew, was a charmer; tall and rangy with curly hair, he'd had a lot of the town girls, and they'd all been waiting for him to come back. Now his eyes were buggy and his voice high like a girl's.

Odysseus said nothing. The mewling yelps, sweet and melodious like a baby pup's, laced through their ears like a thread. It should have been disarming and affectionate. Instead, it became menacing, due to the volume of the sound, loud and booming, like it was coming from a creature seven feet tall.

"I don't know about this," the man with the black beard stubble said, head swiveling around as if the threat could come from anywhere. "We ought to, maybe, go another way."

The redheaded kid was nodding, his arms quivering. "I can't see anything. I feel something bad's coming."

Odysseus shook his head. "We keep going. On through here. This is the way."

His armor shone in the sun and reflected off the rocks. He felt very tall and very powerful up here. The men groaned, but kept rowing.

On the other side of them was another rock, not reaching to the heavens as the first did, but instead lower down, and there was a fig tree, slumped and withered, alien out here in the sea. It was the first thing in their field of vision for, maybe, a split second. Then they saw the black whirling pit of sea. Or, maybe, it wasn't even sea. Maybe it was just a hole in the world.

The pit was spitting and snarling like a deranged ox. There were spittles and fountain-licks of black water shooting up like sparks from a fire. The sound was so alien and so loud that they were all covering their ears. The boat was slowing, with the lack of their rowing motions.

"What the fuck is that?" one man shouted.

"Charybdis," Odysseus said, but maybe he was too quiet, because at that moment, the high-pitched puppy noise got exponentially louder, and turned, imperceptibly, into a shriek, piercing and maniacal.

And Odysseus didn't see it for a second, just heard a series of high screams, but then the boat was rocking back and forth like it was caught in a whirlwind, and there was blood falling from the sky and there were spindling, twisting shadows overhead. Odysseus looked up and could barely describe what he saw. The heads were all the size of boulders he'd seen on mountaintops, all of them wide open to rows of sharp, glistening teeth, slick with blood, the men turning to torn husks in the mouths, flesh grinding between the teeth.

The blood was falling in the water, making contours. There were six of the heads, and they all had beady eyes that seemed like Odysseus was looking into the face of oblivion, deeper and more menacing than anything he'd seen in the depths of the Hades cave.

The men left in the boat were all screaming. There were six empty spots where the oars just hung swinging faintly in the breeze.

Odysseus stared up at the high cave where the heads were now angling toward the sun. He wondered what it must be, to exist so close to the sun. Did it make the monster closer to a God?

~~~

The sounds of the beast's teeth, crunching and grinding flesh, organ and bones, filled the air and the smell, rotten and acrid, seemed to permeate the entire sky. It was no longer so beautiful. Now, it was a stale and horrific place. The men's faces had turned green. Odysseus looked ahead. He didn't feel he could face them.

He could hear their voices, as the ship sailed on past the horrific duopoly of beasts.

"That was Euchares, who got taken. Best bud of mine since we were kids. We used to play in the streets."

"And Noreles, too! He's got a wife and kid at home. Surely, whoever would do this is a monster."

"Poor Lorichus, he just got a promotion at his job back home, too! He was gonna be head of the hunters for feral pigs, a job for which he'd been working for years to get!"

"And there was Antiolus, who was just one stick away from collecting every size and shape of stick in the forest! He was so close! Now, he is monster food! Truly, the person in charge of this is a pig's ass of a man, not fit to be in charge."

They were all afraid, is what it was. They were too cowardly to say his name.

⁓

Eurylochus never liked Odysseus much at all, even back in Ithaca. Even less so, now. Eurylochus came from more modest means. His house had only one gorgeous veranda where the sun shone on the white tile, and he had only three strong horses and only five slaves who picked and killed food for his family's magnificent feasts. But Odysseus had always looked down on him. Odysseus with his royalty and blessing by the gods. Who did he think he was?

Eurylochus thought his whole life had just been a trudge of waiting around for the gods to notice him. He felt he was always out of the spotlight. The gods did not send him prophecies. Nor did they reward his battles won with anything that would set him apart. He knew he would not be written about in the annals of history.

⁓

They were coming to an island, they saw. It was lush and green. This was what Odysseus had been told by Circe. There was blinding white sand before them and the trees stretched up like mountains, looking like one singular mass of shades of green. The men's spirits brightened a little. They were still saddened by the loss of their men but this kind of natural, serene beauty was able to level things a little bit, and although he could not meet their eyes yet, he heard them murmuring among themselves, more contented than before, even if that wasn't saying much. And this was the worst part, because he had to break their hearts.

"We can't stop," Odysseus said.

At this, there were numerous outcries, rising up like puffs of smoke. And it was Eurylochus who spoke up, of course. Odysseus turned to them and saw Eurylochus' blazing eyes, his muscles all tense. The man would fight him if he could get away with it, he knew.

"Hey, you dick," Eurylochus said. "Why can't we stop? We get it – you're the big man, immortal, a hero and shit. You get to stand at the front of the ship and wear your shiny armor. But the rest of us, you know, we're tired. We're hungry. We've barely gotten to sit on dry land for days now. The rowing is hurting our arms."

"Not that we're, you know, weaklings or anything," another man piped up, and Eurylochus gave him a death glare.

Eurylochus continued: "So who're you to say we can't stop there? Have a heart. I know it's hard for you to relate to us common peons. But let us rest a bit."

He looked in their eyes and saw the great need, the masses coalescing, and he relented.

—⁓—

As they were coming closer to the island, the smell of fresh bread and fruits and the sounds of cows mooing rising on the sea, one man said, "Yeah, it looks pretty, but what if there's another monster there?"

"Shut up, Castilles," another guy said. "God, you're always such a bummer."

Odysseus cleared his throat and turned to them, finally meeting their eyes. "Yes, it should be fine. There is just the one thing this time. We're not to eat the cows that live on this island. If you see any cows, you're to leave them alone, or else the gods will rain wrath down upon us."

They were looking confused. One man shrugged. "No big deal."

"We'll be fine." Odysseus puffed his chest out, tried to stretch his arms so he could seem bigger. "We still have a bounty of food from Circe's mansion. It should last us the proper amount of time until we have to leave. And besides, without the six men who got eaten by the monster, well, we ought to be just fine on food rations."

At this, their faces fell again. God dammit, Odysseus thought.

───◦───

So they reached the shores and mounted their ship the best they could, tying it down. Eurylochus watched Odysseus leading the way, not even considering that they could've had some input. The man just considered himself the leader no matter what. Eurylochus thought it arrogant. He yearned for a more democratic form of decision making. He'd thought about this several times; it kept him awake while the rest slept. He thought it would be a better world if the people had more of a say. But any time he voiced this opinion, everyone looked at him as if he had two heads and green, mottled, spiked skin. So he had learned to keep quiet for most of the time.

Now they walked on the sands and Odysseus was reminding them again not to eat the cows. It made Eurylochus want to eat one. Suddenly a nice, fat slab of beef sounded like exactly the right thing.

───◦───

It seemed they'd barely gotten their bearings when the storm started up.

The skies turned black and the wind began to blow, a horrible howling, as if the world was at the mercy of some kind of great wolf.

They would ride out the storm for a week, dining on fruit and bread and wine from Circe's house. The men talked among themselves about their childhoods and their dreams. Their childhoods had been unspectacular. Playing in the dirt as the castles and mansions of the rich loomed in the far distance. They'd entered the service young, enduring backbreaking labor, because they needed to help their families, a sick father, a mother gone, a sister with a broken arm. The army had been the way to do it. Odysseus listened to them. He had not asked them about their pasts before. It was interesting, he supposed.

For the future, they all said they wanted to settle down with a beautiful whore somewhere. Some big mansion somewhere, with a view of the sea, some said, or for others on top of a tall mountain where there'd be mists at their feet in the morning. Maybe some servants of their own.

Then one man took pause, scratching at his unruly curly hair. "But how are we any different, then, we get servants for us?"

Another shrugged. "Just how it is if you get there."

"Big if, I think."

Outside, the world looked as though the dark had become permanent, all swathes of purple sky and streaks of jagged indigo, the trees, blowing like paper in the furious wind. The wind was practically visible now. There was no silence anymore. The sound had filled every crevasse and it was angry.

The next morning, the sun was invisible through the blanket of grey, and the men, despite their full bellies and their wine-tipsy heads, felt a pall of gloom falling over them. Odysseus stood at the mouth of the cave and wondered what the stopping point was here.

"Some island, am I right?" One of the men tried to stand, but the wine and the gluttony had him toppling; he hit the ground. "Wasn't it supposed to be, like, the Isle of the Sun God? What a misleading name."

No one laughed, and his words and his form both seemed to shrink. The cave had a way of doing that, of making them all seem exactly what they were.

Finally, Odysseus told them he was wandering out through the winds. He would prey to Zeus if he had to. The island was wholly untamed, and the only houses had been the ones for the shepherd back near the shore. Odysseus wondered how the shepherd was holding up. He thought it very unfair for the shepherd. The poor man likely hadn't done anything to offend Zeus, likely barely knew the man.

He came to a clearing. There were sagging trees in the rain and the fruit was soaked. The wind howled and bit at his bare flesh. He squinted; it was a very unpleasant way to journey forward. He knelt down there in the damp grass as the wind tried to take bites out of him. He put his head down and spoke in the low voice of prayer.

"Zeus, why'd you have to do this to us? Was it not enough for you to strand us so far from home in the war? What more do we have to suffer? I mean, it's real annoying. It's starting to feel like you really don't like us, and that would hurt my feelings. So, c'mon, man. Can't we remember the good times? Go back to the way things were?"

And he looked to the wind and could see shapes there almost. Dancing, ephemeral shapes, as large as mythological beasts and contorting into forms. It seemed Zeus was considering it.

And a kind of strange rush of rage flowed through Odysseus then. He was out here putting himself at the mercy of a god, humbling himself, admitting that there were greater things at play. And what did he get in return? More wind in his face. It made him feel that nothing he'd done, the war and the bloodshed and the killing of giants, had been worth it at all. And Poseidon was angry over the blinding of his son. Sure. But it had become necessary. Did the big oaf not understand that he was a god and they were all just men? Ants, proportionately, running and scrambling in the dust compared to the gods? What did he expect, for them not to do anything at all?

It was seeming less and less worth it, he thought, to worship these gods. Like petulant children, they acted, he thought. He sat down by a tree. His eyelids were heavy now, and sleep came like a benefactor, a benevolent friend, the world becoming hazy and losing focus.

Eurylochus looked out at the storm. The men had been drawing on the walls of the cave. They'd played word games and guessing games, and had spent a considerable amount of time talking about what the best bird to cook would be. They were imagining up a feast, then. All kinds of exotic arrangements, all the peacocks and wildebeests they could find, and wine that would get you drunker than anything else. These men, famished now, their food running out, were nothing but fantasizing about meals they'd never have, meals that were so far beyond anything they'd get on that rickety old boat, where the wood creaked wetly beneath their feet, where the sails seemed to groan like old war veterans and the oars were brittle now, damp always with the foam and the substance of the sea.

Eurylochus cleared his throat and stood up. "Men, we're dying here." The men went on among themselves, chattering and ruminating and drinking the last sips of wine that was running out. Eurylochus squinted at them. The wind howled behind them, albeit it was something they'd gotten used to now.

The Wine-Dark Sea by Larry Griffin

He cleared his throat again, louder, more exaggerated. At this one, they finally looked up. "Odysseus hasn't been seen all day. He's wandered off and left us here to rot. Did he ever even care?"

"Yeah!" they all shouted in a chorus, as if they'd been practicing.

"And he wanted us not to eat a cow," Eurylochus continued, feeling a stirring in him, a power that hadn't been there before. "What's he doing, though? That prick's probably eating a cow right now. Laughing in our faces, while we're running out of food."

"Yeah!" Another raucous cry. They were with him. He felt a stab of pride.

"Let's go get us a cow! Let's feast mightily like kings! Let's fulfill your dreams of a feast!"

～

And so they walked into the wind. The sky was the color of dark obsidian and the wind was cold, but not so cold that they were deterred, or that the fire in their collective guts went out. They walked down the slope and toward the shore, where the little house where the swineherd lived sat, defiant in the storm, having braved worse. The men spotted the cow they wanted almost instantly; a hefty heifer, staring blankly ahead, chewing on a piece of grass. The wind did not seem to deter the cow. It simply stood, a being existing in the world, and its formidable hide seemed to suggest it would be the choice pick.

They stood there hesitant. Helius, the swineherd, was nowhere to be found.

"Maybe he's out walking or something," one of the men said.

"Just wait," Eurylochus said. "Wait and make sure there's nobody."

But no one came. So the men surrounded the cow and put a stone dagger through its head. It was on the ground and they tore the skin from the cow, bone and tendons pink and glistening. They covered the bones with fat and raw meat, which seemed to shine in the dim, just-returning sunlight. In the absence of any wine, they used water to soak the meat, and added some leaves from the surrounding oaks as barley.

When they began to roast the meat, the smell stung their nostrils in a pleasant way, the fire reaching the sky. They used the remainder of the meat for skewers, putting it on tiny sharpened slivers of bone. They made do with every inch of the cow. Eurylochus looked on what they'd done and felt like he had finally accomplished something.

Odysseus found the cave empty and his gut sank. The wind was dying down to some acceptable level, now, and he strolled as though he were just appreciating the surroundings. He went down the gravel path and then he could see the ocean, rolling waves but sparkling all the same, the sun illuminating the surface like it was glass, and it went on forever, just on and on.

But then his eyes focused on what was before him.

He couldn't tell what it was at first. It just looked like a collection of blood-scarlet-shaded lumps. It smelled, too, of burnt-out fire and the fly and maggot-ridden waste of death, pungent and repulsive. He stepped closer and realized it was all of Helius' cows, all laid out now like trash heaps. The men were lying in the shade of an oak, sleeping and smiling, hands over their ample bellies.

When they awoke, they saw his disappointed face, his stern eyebrows, his mouth turned down in a scowl. He stood there with his arms crossed and was as much like a god as anything they'd seen. Most of them had lived among the plebeians and everyone seemed a god to them.

On the ship, a dark cloud, the purest shade of midnight, rolled toward them like a snail. It was making a rumbling sound every bit as menacing as that which had been emitted by Charybdis, that awful whirlpool. The men rowed, but there were murmurs of discontent among them. "I don't think I want to go toward that," one said.

"Well, you should've thought about this when you ate those cows," Odysseus said, standing on the prow. His own stomach groaned. He hadn't eaten since the last of Circe's food, from the cave. His long sleep had made him irritable, and his throat was dry.

"Hey, I just figured it would be kind of an appropriate punishment, you know?" the man said. "I thought it'd be, like, a hangnail. Or maybe I'd never be able to sleep in a very comfortable way."

"No, we've angered Zeus," Odysseus said, casting his eyes to the bulbous cloud, which swelled with crackling, phantasmagorical light, all ethereal yellow-white and even pink, looking as hot as the sun. The air felt like it had a friction to it, like any moment it could explode into flame like one of the pyres they buried their dead upon. The wind that glided, snake-like, over the waves was low and groaning. The sound reminded them of crypt-wind.

Odysseus looked in the clouds and, if he stared at the right angle, he could see Zeus' face, the eyebrows furrowed, eyes blazing red like hot coals, mouth a swollen blister of fury.

LARRY GRIFFIN

Larry Griffin is a writer from Florida, raised on a diet of horror movies, heavy metal music and crime literature. When not writing or performing stand-up comedy, he can be found at a beach or a movie theater.

Mad Mad Captain Ahab

Moby Dick

John Di Donna

Call him Queequeg.
"There! There she be!"

Captain Ahab, by now a permanent fixture on the top deck, only sleeping while still standing upright, stirred to life. "What mean ye by that, harpooner? I've the rancid smell of the beast in my nostrils, have ye eyes on that infernal mark or haven't ye?"

"Aye, Captain," said the cannibal, descending down the ratlines of the foremast from his lookout perch, "But she be blowin' no more!"

~

The Pequod, that dread claw-footed slaughterhouse, followed the pillar of sea birds that funneled above a great white plateau that broke the endless expanse of sea, and was brought alongside yon buoyant cadaver.

Certainly it was he, the object of the Captain's wild vindictiveness, the ever elusive, nigh mythologic Moby Dick, identifiable by his deformed jaw, the arcane wrinkled brow, and the unharvested wheat field of harpoons still embedded in his flanks. Of the three prominent punctures of the flukes, there were no sign, as the lower half of the animal was missing entirely, the entrails of beast torn apart and drifting free in the current. Not dissimilar to an angler drawing up a smaller catch, only to have it struck at the water's surface by a larger predator, there Moby Dick floated, cleft in two by an unthinkable cavernous maw, or by gargantuan appendages.

Silence fell across the port decks, all hands tongue tied in the thrall of the anti-climax, almost reverent in mourning for the magnificence of said beast, paranoid to the nature of the unfathomable fiend that very well still may lurk just beneath the ship's keel, and most fearfully, awaiting the reaction of their fanatical Captain.

"Dam me eyes, me bet dis means dat dere be no gold coin for old-e Queequeg!"

Those within earshot looked at the islander as if he had a death wish, but Ahab paid him no heed, only stared fixedly upon the mutilated whale meat bobbing in the surf. The only one to react was the cabin boy Pip, who had become the embodiment of nervousness, rescued not once but twice from the immensity of the ocean, its slithering unspeakable shapes sliding just beneath him crippling his very wellness of being.

The laugh of Bedlam on his lips, the doomed youth sang out, "Who's seen worthless Pip? Here he is, I've found him, haha, for all the blackness of his living skin, he still sucks the air! But what does Pip's eyes see before him, none but what Hell has spat back out, Job's white washed Leviathan feeding the fishes!" The demonic sounds of pixies frolicking broke free from his lips, chilling the men to their core. "And so does black live and white perishes. How now our Captain? Will the rest of him now die with this whale, and be as dead as his lost leg?"

The deranged words struck sparks upon the tinder of the Captain's flinty heart.

"Shall the Pequod be naught but a funeral procession for my late nemesis? Look alive, me hearts, Moby Dick won't be inviting himself on board tonight. Make haste, and salvage what ye can. Mr. Stubb, eat your fill, but bring me the devil's eyes and his most foul heart, those are mine and mine alone. Mr. Starbuck, we'll be underway as soon as the labor's finished."

"Aye, Captain, once again back 'round the Cape and back to our purveyors, then!"

Ahab stopped his stride, as if struck. "Nay, chief, our work here is far from completed."

The crew at the fore lowered to the water, and made ready the preparations to save what they could from what the sharks and the seagulls had left for them. But those within earshot of the staff's voices stopped, the tension creeping across the deck like a thing alive.

"Insufferable! Captain, I've circumnavigated this firmament by thine side, obeying thine blasphemous commands, my every action a sleight to God in heaven, e'en as I've served thee as I do He, but this fight is fought, the race is run. Moby Dick now lies forever undone at your feet."

"Know this, my fine bilge filth, no member of this crew will know his home until we find a home in Hell for what unnamed creature such as makes Moby Dick his plaything!" As the spark's of Pip's words did ignite all that was vile and vindictive in Ahab's breast, so now did Ahab's words ignite the quarter deck as if it'd been soaked in oil.

"God and thunder, man!" Starbuck snapped. "League after league I knew what blackened your heart. This has nothing to do with your late whale, or anything other godforsaken fish that e'er swam in the sea, it never did, even from the first day that thunderstruck gold was nailed to the tree!"

"Mind that treacherous tongue before it suffers the same fate as this leg."

Second mate Stubb bristled, suddenly at Starbuck's side. "Aged, wicked old man. That leg of yours has haunted my dreams for the entirety of this voyage! It's well time you put it up, Captain, and let the good work of guiding this ship home fall to us!"

"Ho! Such a mutinous row from the mangiest of dogs! Treacherous Judas, striking your Captain at his lowest!"

Defying his gristled appearance, Ahab lashed out, his ivory leg brought up and let to fly straight across Stubb's midriff, in time with the rising pitch of the ship, knocking him backward and over the gunwale. Shock froze Starbuck where he was, before the panic of Stubb unprotected in waters surging with sharks prodded him to action. Ahab leapt at him, denying Starbuck's assistance, and dealing him an ivory clad stomp that nearly crushed the bones of his foot, dropping the chief to the deck in pain.

Queequeg sprung forward, his ever present harpoon in hand, the speed of a panther his to command. The head of his spear found a loop of a whale line, and before anyone could so much as inhale enough breath to shout after him, he was atop the rail, and hurling his weapon down at Stubb.

Ishmael was agog for what seemed the hundredth time since befriending his cannibalistic companion. Did this island prince mean to inflict a mercy killing? It was not to be, with the precision he'd been revered for, Queequeg struck the waves north of Stubb's bobbing head, parting his hair, and trailing the rescue line within his grasp. A voyage plagued with swamped whaleboats and failed rescues, the Maori warrior would not see more death while he had breath to prevent it.

Barking his Polynesian patois, he commanding every able body within reach to haul as if Stubb's life depended on it. Queequeg himself did not;

rather, he took up a second dart and stood akimbo between the line and the Captain, his eyes searching the waters for sharks hungering for living prey, yet intoning that interfering with the rescue would be most unwise.

Three darts flew, each felled a toothy predator that lusted after Stubb.

Starbuck rose to his feet, making noise about attempted murder and unfitness to command. Ahab cut him off.

"Look! Open those useless eyes and look on the remains of our once proud fugitive! See the lacerations across the anterior flanks, the trauma along the lines of incision? Have you in all your days seen such unbridled power? Now, imagine turning tail and abandoning the hunt, leaving such a rogue predator as that unchecked, to prey on any artless vessel. And thou calls thyself a Christian!" Ahab bristled, as if selling himself on the notion as well as his Quaker chief, coming to accept it as truth he'd just created.

Stubb was hauled up, a half dozen pair of hands helping him to his feet, soaked and bruised, looking to his mates to see where everyone stood.

"Mr. Stubb, the next time the mood for a bit of recreation strikes thee, please attempt to do so on thine own time. Now, there's sperm to cook and oil to barrel, step to it!"

Spade poles and blubber hooks flashed and rent dead flesh, men transformed into carpenter ants, swarming the remains of the albino whale, consuming him down to his last. Ishmael, however, paused in his sweat-soaked labors, staying his boarding sword, taking in the sight that was the late beast's head. The skin of many a baleen was scored with ligatures, both naturally borne and battle scarred both, but the markings that covered the white whale's hide seemed deliberately drawn by some ungodly hand.

"By my soul, how ill equipped is unlettered Ishmael to decipher such damnable Chaldee engraved here like fine Italian craftsmanship. Will no one here take note, let alone decode and transcribe what this mystic-marked whale is saying?" None answered, the fear coming off the beast as palpable as its blubbery mass, as consuming as the sea of blood spilled across the timbers.

Mad Mad Captain Ahab by John Di Donna

Ahab's dusky phantoms, the aboriginal Manilan natives once concealed below deck for the duration of the voyage, now were everywhere, tending to their diabolic machinations with the same dedication every deckhand had for their daily ablutions. Fedallah, the Captain's tiger yellow secretive confidant, strapped himself to the bowsprit and remained there for the perpetuation, a profane imitation of Odin on the World Tree, his cries and incantations a spectral siren call cast out to the immeasurable depths. The nameless other four enacted what had heretofore only been the subject of fantastical stories upon the page; stoking burning braziers with noxious formulas and billowing fumes, scribing star movements across the whole of the deck with sharp pikes, navigating uncharted leagues with compasses crafted from blood-quenched harpoons, performing mortification of their own flesh with whip and flail, and feasting on the raw sweetbreads of whale cadaver.

Nor did they concentrate solely on the skies and the ship, but also on the sailors themselves, plying them with strange liquors drawn from fire-blackened barrels, or entrancing them with pipes stuffed with Turkish kief and Arabian poppies.

The skies bled red both at dusk as well as dawn, much to the mariners' consternation. One such bloodstained gloaming, the purgatorial band summoned forth both Captain and crew atop the waist deck, the braziers belching forth brimstone and spermaceti stoked flames, transforming the Pequod into an undiscovered level of Hell that Dante had yet to attend.

Suspended from the cutting tackle was the heart of Moby Dick, as large as any four able bodied men. The eyes, not half as monstrous as the monster itself, about the size of a steer's, sat on either side of the serpentine circlet inscribed on the deck. The profane quartet knelt at each of the compass points, intoning and chanting, employing a daemoniac consecration upon their most recent labors, a new leg, hewn from the ivory jawbone of the white whale himself.

From the darkness of the aftcastle, an apparition appeared, one who could only be mad Captain Ahab, but as unlike in appearance to his former self as life was from death. Stripped bare to his breeches, his hair and beard splayed forth, creating a wispy corona about his skull. He now bore the same scrimshaw etchings transplanted from the fated whale's corpse, covering him from scalp to stump. The collective intake of breath from the crew caused the sails to snap on their spars.

Divesting himself of his old leg, he heaved the prosthetic into the closest brazier, scattering profanities as well as cinders across the deck. The ghastly trio bade him to lay prone whist the fourth rose with his ivory burden, and went about the task of tempering the brass fittings over the open fire. The cast metal glowering white hot in the twilight, he bade his comrades to restrain the Captain and hold him fixed.

"Belay that order! Take thine filthy devil hands from off my personage!" blustered Ahab. "Moby Dick robbed me of my leg, but hath left my manhood intact. Do your worst, pit-spawn, there's no pain you can inflict upon the remains of this body that it hast not already borne!" They obeyed, and with no hesitation, the phantom harpooner thrust the molten metal upon the severed stump. All that was Ahab writhed, as tormented as Christ on His cross, but he pulled not away from that immolation.

The four were up on their feet, harpoons hefted, and by some unspoken command, stabbed the hanging heart in unison. Blood issued forth, dank and sour, quenching the blazing bronze, bonding it forever with the Captain's flesh with a seal of scarification.

<hr />

Bets were taken as to how long before infection ate away at such a grievous wound suffered upon the Captain. Stubb was of the theory that Fedallah was the incarnation of the Devil himself, and meant to take command of the Pequod as soon as Ahab shrugged free of his mortal coil, and then ferry his soul down to Hades, along with rest of the assembled personnel. Yet, all wagers were off as the doors to the officer's cabins were flung wide, and who should storm across the top deck with the stride of Hannibal crossing the Alps, but the mad Captain himself, his leg miraculously, nay, daemonically healed.

His vengeance-laden voice summoned all hands to attend him, in his hands, the death tempered harpoon intended to play the role of the headman's axe in Moby Dick's execution. The memory of its forging from horse shoe nails and barbed from the Captain's razors, then baptized in the blood of the pagans Queequeg, Tashtego, and Daggoo, was still freshly tattooed in their memories. Across the surface, newly inscribed sigils and symbols had been engraved, alien, Hyperborean scrivenings none aboard could begin to understand, save the shadowy assassins.

"The song of mine brethren's' voices, the day this weapon was crafted by my own hands, still sings out loud in my heart of hearts!" Ahab cried. "Remember now, thine blood bound oaths, the night I'd channeled the lightning and tamed the thunders." Laying the head of the harpoon down on the coals of the perpetually stoked firepots, he continued. "Fire forged steel is weapon enough against a mortal enemy such as Moby Dick, but now, my hearts, we face he who would hunt the hunted, who would kill the killer, the incarnation of everything loathsome and harrowing that the depths of the Abyss has birthed forth, he whom even the Biblical Behemoth fears and flees. Be ye mine arrows in my hand, fill mine quiver with thine very souls! For even the pagans among thee are sparked with the Creator's spirit, and so shall I lay ye down on the anvil and shape you anew in a refining fire!" And, in a retelling of the events of the night before, did Ahab retrieve the searing firebrand, and drew it to his chest, as a mother does a newborn babe. His screams of agony turned to peals of laugher, he having burned away what was left of his sanity.

"Ho! Starbuck! Servant of the Lord and prophet to the nations! Wherefore art thine Shadrach, Meshach and Abednego now? Come forth and walk with them through the heart of the inferno!" The laughter that escaped his still smoking chest cavity contained nothing of the holy about it.

The divinations at the hands of the phantom's ethereal astrolabes brought the Pequod to the remotest points of the Pacific, aligned along the same laterals as the Easter Islands thousands of miles to the east.

No one could say exactly when Fedallah's excoriating vigil had become fatal. But having been found dead, the remaining four Manilans rejected a burial at sea, and instead fixed his corpse to the ship's toothed jaw-bone tiller, the better to guide them across the River Styx. On any other ship, a gruesome trophy, but on the Pequod, already bestrewn fore to aft with the bones of its slain enemies, just another harbinger of the deaths yet to come.

The entirety of the crew had been anti-Christened in one of two fashions, either by a branding with newly forged harpoon heads of their own, or, to those who found such procedures a heresy not to be endured, taking the Polynesian tatau markings at the hands of the cannibal Queequeg.

As son of the king, full authority was in his hands to indoctrinate anyone he deemed worthy into his tribe, inscribing them with benedictions to his pagan deity Yojo, and with the histories of his forbearers. Each sailor rested atop Queequeg's recently commissioned coffin as the work was tapped in, using tools fashioned from the same shark's teeth that he'd killed the day he'd saved Stubb's life.

"You saved me from the jaws of death once before, Islander, I have faith that ye can do it again!" To Ishmael's shame, it was Stubb who was first to be so carved, his skin now more black than white.

The lone outlier was chief officer Starbuck, who'd rather lose the whole of his body than have his soul flung into Hell.

⌒

Volcanic red rose across the horizon, another omen of chasing the same fate that befell Moby Dick. The whole of his tatau labors complete, Queequeg rose up to challenge his unseen adversary, his best weapons of bravery and courage at hand. Taking to the forecastle, he stomped his feet, beat his breast, and thrashed about in a fearsome pantomime, performing the fierce-some Haka of his people.

The second day, he rose to greet the dawn with his war dance, and was joined by Ishmael.

The third day, by Stubb.

The fourth, by old King Post Flask himself.

And so did they sojourn through the southern climes, until Queequeg had the whole of the crew chanting and howling to the heavens, from every deck across the vessel, as if to strike terror into the heart of Death herself.

⌒

The final day, the sky cleared of crimson, and the most beautiful day in all of their collected lives welcomed them.

Midmorning, there was a tremor, the kind of seismic shaking one encounters on dry land when earthquakes level cities. The whole of the sea convulsed, a great concussion erupting from the firmaments.

All on deck could see it, but those spies perched at the mastheads had the best view; a shadow, the size of an atoll, came from behind at speed, passing under the Pequod, seemingly without incident. The sheer mass of such a shade struck the crew-mates dumb. Before anyone could speak out and offer up a theorem, there was a breach, such like no man aboard had ever witnessed, save perhaps in the arctic climes, when a mountain range of glacial ice broke free and avalanched into the sea.

For an incalculable forever, it hung aloft, its mind-bending immensity dwarfing the late great whale Moby Dick by degrees, a colossus the size of three frigates jumping in tandem. What it was escaped any known conventional categorization, but whatever it was, it was no whale.

The foremost expanse was an amalgamation of bathypelagic species and frilled amphibians, its skeletal system jutting out at impossible angles from a ram shaped mantle, slimy and scaly both, rimmed with undulating swim ribbons, probing antennae, and protruding eye stalks. Bulbous siphons prolapsed and spawned toothed maws that mimicked the lamprey's. The hindquarters of the beast shared the combined properties of the colossal squid, the nautilus, and the cuttlefish, the base of the mantle aligned with directional flukes, giving way to an arsenal of spine covered tentacles.

With the sound of the world ending just off the port bow, the impossibility thundered back down into the ocean, displacing so much seawater as to create a spontaneous squall, and caveating the surface with its own localized tidal waves.

As the mere shadow of the Brobdingnagian nightmare had silenced the crew, the sight of that shadow's maker had struck them senseless, their fight and will to live stripped clean from their souls. Not King Post, who'd bragged of lowering during full gales, nor Queequeg, who'd taken his first head at puberty, nor even the flint-hearted phantoms could so much as speak, let alone spur the least part of themselves to action. There was only one, a soul out-crier raising his voice in the face of certain destruction.

Mad mad Ahab.

"At last does my cold dead heart beat again in my chest, beats forth the drumbeat of thine funeral march, most foul and detestable abomination!"

Sprinting cross deck, Ahab moved as if his ivory peg had been his since birth, charging to the front of the prow, arming himself as he flew. As the nose of the Pequod pitched skyward in the wake of the cyclonic disturbance, the creature crested, slinging between the waves in the most whale-like fashion. With no hesitation, Ahab fired his harpoon with the concussive force of a canon, burying the barb in the foul, putrid flesh.

The dart held, and coils of whale line leapt up and followed the aberration overboard.

"HA! First blood to Ahab!" Fists in the air, he roared at the crew, commanding them to storm the front line, insisting that this was just another damnable fish to be taken from the sea.

The first round of darts found their target, (although to miss such a target as that would be like trying to ram a vessel into a continent, and missing), the whale lines fixed, the Pequod then was transformed from globe spanning tall ship to lowered whaling longboat, as the titanic beast descended and dragged them along. Such was the power of their latest quarry, that the Pequod plowed the sea, sinking deep, well past the cargo holds and mid-decks, far closer to the water line than e'er should be, the waist deck awash in surf, a wake carved through the ocean like ruts through muddy earth.

Another volley of blood-tempered barbs darkened the air at each sounding, striking their intended, until the mass of lines fixing the craft to the prey became a hempen tangle.

"Drop anchor! Drop the drogues!" commanded Ahab. A delay, as the dazed and confused crew-mates comprehended the orders, then moving briskly to comply. Anchors the size of whale skulls and chains with link the size of a ribcage plunged into the brine, adding additional drag and pull to the creature's burden.

A few leagues sloughed by without any signs of the beast slowing or sounding. "Helmsman!" Ahab bellowed to the quarterdeck. "Hard aport, now!" The pilot on the tiller threw his all into the jawbone, setting the rudder as far over as he was able, the Pequod heaving against the surf at speeds it had never witnessed on its own. Ahab's stratagem had its effect, that of all the barbs inside that pusillanimous flesh being heaved against all at once. "Helmsman! Hard starboard, now!" The stunt was repeated; the Pequod again arching across the path of the beast, and this time the dropforged barbs tore through and flew free. "On your guard, me hearts, take in those lines, prepare those darts for another pass!"

The phantoms appeared next to the men who drew the harpoons home, and re-baptised them, pulling them across their own flesh and letting them drink blood anew. The edges of the blades glowed with thaumaturgic energies, and when they were fired again, they crackled the sonic discharge of lightning before a strike. The sharpshooters, the pagans and the Manilans, plied their trade with such acumen, selecting bull's-eyes that may have been sensory organs or weaknesses along the flanks, scoring direct hits, and being rewarded with bellows from beneath.

"Sails aback! Head cloth across the weather sheet! Come, me boys tack hard!"

The abysmal beast slowed, and rising to the surface, let its terrible ten tacles loosed upon the Pequod. Blows pummeled the timbers like cannon ball grapeshot, taloned spines tore and gouged, and the whipcrack from a looming tendril snapped the upper spar of the foremast, only the cat's cradle of rigging saving it from dropping on the crew's heads.

All hands gave as good as they got, employing all of the butchery tackle and blubber spades as if just another day of harvest. Footing became a precious commodity, the decks slick with blood and ichor, the ship heaving in the churning maelstrom beneath their keel.

~

They continued like this, replaying the same battle-scarred cycles, until well into the watches of the night. The braziers blazed, the furnaces stoked, the blacksmith and the phantoms made a run of the ship's stores to the point of depletion, fashioning new iron to add to the arsenal. At the beast's first breach at the dawn, darts still white hot from the forge scorched their paths through the air, striking with a searing squelch on wet flesh, sinking their full length beneath the skin.

After round after round of harpooning and towing, the pythonic mon strosity changed tack and began to circle, making an earnest effort to throw itself free from it shackles. Ahab, at the helm, whipped the tiller, sending the ship careening up over the wall of the wake, the tension of the lines screaming out a taught catgut cry. Heaving the jawbone back, the Pequod dipped, its spinnaker poles catching hold of the surf, digging the craft deeper into the depths below the waterline. Whether fatigued or merely annoyed, the beast twisted back upon itself with the gyrations of a distended sea cucumber, causing the waters beneath the ship to writhe, the craft hurtling aloft on the storming surge.

The keel nearly vertical against the sky, Ahab hauled with inhumane strength, and pivoted the vessel into free-fall. "Anchors up!" called the Captain, the mates scrambling against the hard angles of the pitched deck to the capstans, breaking their backs in efforts to comply and retract the chains.

Bellowing his sadistic war cry, Queequeg dove headfirst from the top deck, and hurled himself at the monstrosity below. This incited a wave of kamikaze attacks; he was joined in the melee by a number of the harpooners. They struck their marks with surgical precision, slicing through gill slits, impaling nictitating eyeballs, and carving holes with blubber spades wide enough for the condemned seamen to bury themselves inside the monster's barnacled flesh.

Following in Queequeg's strides, Ahab piloted the vessel into a nose-dive, accelerating madly across the cresting tidal wave, and training the cusp of the bowsprit at the beast's most vulnerable orifice.

The impact of ship to flesh was volcanic.

Every beam and spar of the Pequod quaked and threatened to tear itself apart from the ship, as the bowsprit lanced its way deep into the quivering Leviathan, the lecherous ichor that served as the abomination's lifeblood spewed forth from its newly drilled blowhole. Gargantuan and galleon both wailed in agony, the tentacles flagellating and lashing forth as if each were possessed by its own personal demon, the ship's masts snapping mid-spar and falling free, miles of snaking hemp and spider webbed rigging serving to entangle the beast all the more as it engaged in a one-sided tug of war.

The keel folded in on itself, and flung the aftcastle forward to meet the fore. Ahab released his grip on the tiller, plunging into the fray, a death knell upon his lips, and coming face to face with his quarry, dropped the full length of his peg into the creature's eye. Taking a pair of protrusions in his grasp, Ahab braced himself and continued to stomp, even as the Pequod was torn asunder, coming apart and raining holy terror down upon them both.

Ishmael had been thrown an uncharted distance, catapulted from the imploding foredeck, plunging so deep beneath the briny depths that he felt the pressure threatening to crush the last of his life from his bloody lungs. As darkness spread forth its fingers to embrace him at the last, a swift undercurrent seized him and pulled him forward, and he could see a surging vortex forming as the crippled monstrosity dragged the scuttled ship down in a spiraling death roll, propelling the mariner back up as it dove down.

He had no idea how long he'd been out for, being buoyed aloft by the junkyard flotsam that had shortly been his home vessel for the past year. The waves that lapped against the midspan he clung to were oil slick thick, the pestilent cruor of the nightmarish horror thick atop the sea. He'd been awakened by the impact of a sturdy wooden craft, Queequeg's coffin, bobbing brightly, unaware of the carnage of the aquatic battlefield about it. Scanning the swells, the eddies, and the horizon, Ismael sought out any glimmer of life, and came up wanting.

Then, the tide stirred anew, and Ishmael, who was exhausted beyond the ability to synthesize enough adrenaline to become fearful any longer, resigned himself to a death at the returning creature's hands. But it was not to be.

A legion of shadows swam beneath him, a flurry of the same shadows as when the Leviathan was first sighted, large as sandbars, an entire school flocking to their fallen brother's side.

The notion that there may have been more than one single specimen of the unimaginable sea devil broke the fragile remains of his sanity in two.

Yet, another reality-defying realization came upon him, as the whole of the quadrant swelled and pulsed, raising the debris field up high, higher again than where the topmasts of the fated ship had stood. The cause: a new shadow, one that was no mere tiny atoll or cay, but at a size rivaling a peninsula.

Ishmael slid deep into the embrace of raving madness, as he bore witness to the swarming school of young, mere juveniles, now being reunited with their mother.

John Di Donna

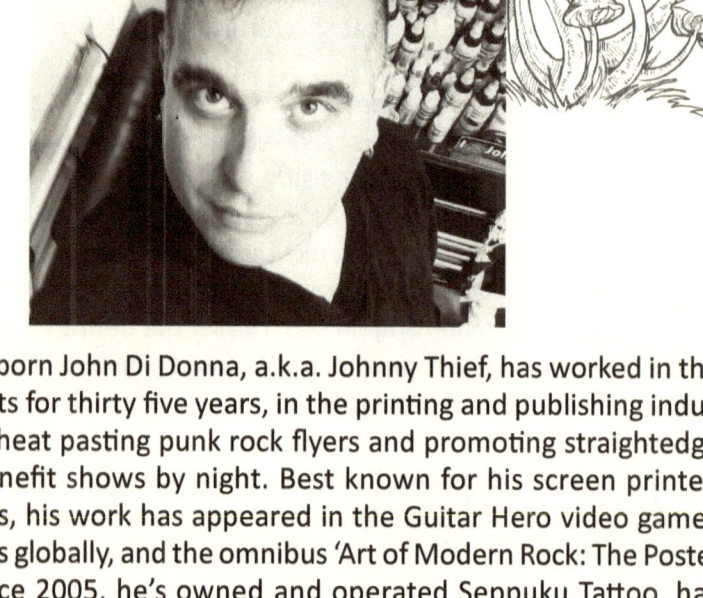

Brooklyn born John Di Donna, a.k.a. Johnny Thief, has worked in the visual arts for thirty five years, in the printing and publishing industries by day, wheat pasting punk rock flyers and promoting straightedge drug rehab benefit shows by night. Best known for his screen printed concert posters, his work has appeared in the Guitar Hero video games, Hard Rock Cafes globally, and the omnibus 'Art of Modern Rock: The Poster Explosion.' Since 2005, he's owned and operated Seppuku Tattoo, has painted covers for industry magazines, and judged contests at tattoo conventions internationally. His first foray into traditional publishing came when he was included in the #1 Amazon best selling horror anthology 'The Monsters We Forgot' (Soteira Press, 2019). An alumn of the Kubert School, a member of The Horror Writers Association, his favorite hobby is giving a fuck.

seppukutattoo.com

facebook.com/johnnythief

@seppukutattoo

TINK'S CHOICE
PETER PAN

Erika Lance

Tink sat on the ledge of the window of the Darling house. She watched as Peter, her Peter, moved even closer to the horrific girl called: Wendy. She wanted to rip Wendy's head off... literally. However, as a fairy she was too small to accomplish the task. In fact, she was too tiny to do much harm at all to a human of almost any size. Peering down at Wendy's youngest brother, Michael, she thought it may be possible to cause him to bleed but it would not do anything to her enemy, Wendy, at all.

Catching movement from the corner of her eye, her attention was drawn back to Peter. She turned in time to see him tenderly move a strand of hair behind Wendy's ear. Her fists clenched as Tink screamed in outrage. She couldn't in-fact scream, not the way a human could. Instead, she sounded more like an angry little bell. Humans could not understand fairies. Tink had often thought it was because humans were unwilling to try hard enough. The human language had been easy for her to understand after a short time.

Tink returned her attention back to Peter, and watching him continue to tenderly interact with Wendy. This was all because Wendy had helped Peter reattach his shadow, which she knew Peter was incredibly grateful for. Although, Tink was sure she could have helped with that same task had she been given the chance. Wendy, the wench, had jumped in before Tink had the opportunity to do anything and this is why Wendy was the absolute worst.

Anger began to rise within her again.

Then her rage boiled to the surface and her cheeks began to flush. Taking a deep breath in and out she came up with a plan. Looking over at Wendy sitting in her nightgown, she resembled a frilly bag of potatoes giggling and talking. Tink realized she could lodge herself in Wendy's throat and block her airway. Make her choke on fairy dust in the most literal of ways until she fell over with blue lips and no life left in her. Peter would surely not be interested in a lifeless corpse.

Narrowing her eyes, she waited for the right moment. Holding the edge of the window frame she readied to launch herself directly into Wendy's mouth the next time it opened. Then, just as Wendy's head flew back and a belly laugh came through her lips, obviously from something Peter had done, as Wendy was super dull, Tink launched into the air, speeding towards her mouth. As she neared her target Wendy suddenly fell back on the bed, still laughing and wrapping her hands around her middle.

Before she could change course, she flew over Wendy at such speed she smacked into the wall, knocking the wind and sense out of her. Finding herself sliding down the wall to the floor in a small heap of pissed off fairy and shimmery dust.

When her vision started to return, she tried to take a breath. Now she was even more angry. She was furious! Peter always told her she couldn't think when she was angry. "Tink" he would say in a soft voice. "You are like a wind-up toy. When you're angry you end up in all directions at once". She loved his voice. She loved his smile. She loved everything about Peter. Her Peter. She started to feel her anger dissipate, until she remembered the one thing she didn't love: Peter having any feelings for Wendy.

Standing slowly, she made sure she wasn't too dizzy to fly. Taking a few breaths, she took off out the window. She did not fly as fast as she could. She was hoping to hear Peter's voice call out to her before she made it very far. Imagining he would ask her where she was going. Tell her he needed her. No such question came. She turned around to see if he were looking toward her retreat, but she could not get angry again. Tink was determined and it needed to stay that way until she got to where she was headed.

Tink had found she could in fact be sidetracked by anything. This was a curse of being a fairy after all. The actions, person, or thing around her only needed to slightly change her emotion, then she would lose track of her previous task or thought. It was in fact quite easy to trap a fairy for this reason. Peter had done just that after all.

For a time, she had convinced Peter that if she did not get enough attention she would simply fade away. She would watch him play with the Lost Boys or outwit the pirates, including Captain Hook, but the moment her emotion turned to jealousy, she would wilt like a flower in front of

Peter and he would race to her side. Now he let her fall to the floor without so much as a glance in her direction.

The stars raced by and she started to remember the first time Peter and she had met. She thought of the first time they had flown together after she had shown him how. She sighed, then shook her head, stopping herself. She needed to concentrate. WENDY! She flew faster. There was someone she needed to see.

It took her a little while to get to the location. Not because it was any farther than the Island of Lost Boys. It was because it was more perilous for a fairy or any creature of the light to travel to. For here was where the darkness lived.

Most did not speak of the Isle of Ilk or the creatures that lived there Dark creatures of nightmares. In fact, even the worst of pirates avoided rolling through its waters. Some even made it appear to be a giant whirl pool on the map so that ships would know to avoid it entirely.

The Isle itself was surrounded by a dark, dense fog. When it you touched your skin, it left a slick, oily residue behind that had a smell like fish that had been beached for days in the hot sun.

As you neared the isle, the temperature also increased dramatically With the moist air, it almost felt as if you were slowed down by its weight

Pausing and listening as she approached, she noticed the sound of waves hitting the beach was missing. The only sound she could hear was a faint buzzing as if off in the distance. She debated turning around. Her determination wavered slightly.

Just then something moved in the fog in front of her. It was fast and pushed past her, almost making contact. Should she turn around?

If she did, what would she find?

Only one thing came to mind: WENDY!

Her rage flared, gulping it back remembering why she was here. She squared her shoulders and launched further into the fog.

The fog seemed to go on forever. She was coated head to toe in the slimy film before suddenly she broke through with a pop. Here the air turned more frigid and drier. She coughed and her lungs burned. There was something in the air here that tasted almost like ash.

As she coughed, dust fell off her to the ground below and she noticed something moving on the ground, collecting it. Floating down, she took a closer look and a tentacle reached up to grab her. She flew, nar rowly missing its grasp as the barbs on the tentacle tore her clothing at the shoulder.

It was silly after all. Clothing. She only wore it because Peter wore clothing. Not that he could tell what she was wearing. He just knew it was green. Bright green to be exact. This seemed to be his favorite color. Tink had started with wrapping a leaf around herself. Although most leaves are smooth to the touch, she found that it was very itchy. Then she used a rose thorn and tore a small piece of bright green fabric from a cape one of the lost boys had found while rummaging around in a trunk that had washed ashore.

She was losing her train of thought again. She needed to focus.

The creature beneath her jutted two tentacles towards her. No wait, three, four, no SIX! There were barbs everywhere. She bobbed and weaved through them as she saw giant maw come into view. It had several rows of very sharp teeth and as she weaved through the mass of sharp edges, she realized it was flying. Or floating.

It was sparkling with fairy dust. She panicked. What had she done?

Then almost as suddenly as the panic set in, she found herself in the dark. Frantic now she wondered if the creature had swallowed her whole. She felt her heart race and knew she needed to get out. She didn't want to be eaten. Would Peter miss her? Did he even know she was gone?

Her thoughts were jumbling. She was starting to become sad. She looked all around trying to find any source of light. When she couldn't find any, she looked to simply find a change in the darkness anywhere. She couldn't see a thing. She started to feel like she was suffocating. There was nowhere to go. Her eyes couldn't focus. Unable catch her breath, was she dying? Panic overwhelmed her and her vision went black.

～～

Something was tapping on her foot then it stopped. Was it an angel? Peter had said that there were creatures with wings, like fairies, but their wings were made out of white feathers and they came for you when you died.

Tap, tap, tap. She felt it again.

She slowly opened her eyes, hoping it was not bright. It wasn't, but she blinked her eyes several times, adjusting them.

When a fairy first wakes up it is a weird time for her. This is because most of the time, you are not feeling anything when you first wake up. Having no memories from the sleep. Peter said "Humans call it dreaming".

Tink liked to believe Peter.

As her vision cleared, she was sitting on a small rock shelf, looking into the face of a cross between a human and a monster. It had greenish grey skin, yellow eyes with no irises, just slits of black like a cat. It had spots on the sides of it's face that looked like large freckles. It smiled, its teeth were sharp and the smile did not bring happiness. It was menacing.

Tink tried to scoot back, but she did not get far before her back was up against something solid.

"It's not dead" the creature said turning to look behind him in the shadows.

"Good" Tink heard an exceptionally smooth voice come out of the darkness. She was instantly intrigued. Her whole body reacted to the voice. It was nothing like she had ever felt before. She found herself wanting to move closer to it.

The creature in front her clawed fingers started to reach for her, and she moved back again. Not realizing how far forward she had come moving towards the voice she had just heard.

It had almost grabbed her when she heard "Let it go Imp. You are scaring her." Tink melted again.

Trying to listen harder for the voice Tink realized she had only felt this emotion once before. It was with Peter.

Peter... Tink wondered if he was missing her... Did he even know she was gone? Or was he still looking at her... at Wendy!

No longer wistful, anger was all she could feel. Standing she began stomping around the small ledge was on. She was here for a reason and she needed to get what she came here for. Looking around a little more, she tried to figure out how to get out this situation. Squinting she tried to make out what was further in the shadows.

As if it had somehow the shadows read her thoughts the darkness peeled itself back and showed she was in a much larger cave then she had first imagined. There were also ledges of various sizes all around with different creatures atop them. She did not see cages, but none of the creatures were moving much. She started to fly up to get a better look but found she could only get so far as something stopped her progress up.

The creature called Imp had almost grabbed her again. How had he done that? She landed and walked towards the edge of the ledge again she was stopped but she felt it this time. Bars. She was in a cage. She had to assume that they all were.

Peering deeper into the cave she saw the monster called Imp. He was sitting on a table where there were many vials and other items she could not make out from this angle. Then she saw someone approach out of the shadows in the back of the cave. He was tall, like Peter. Actually, he was taller than Peter. He had on black pants, boots and was not wearing a shirt. As she looked closer his skin had a subtle glow to it.

He was looking at her. His smile was mesmerizing. She found that couldn't look away from his gaze. She was also no longer angry. In fact, the feeling was that she needed to be touched by him. The man's eyes never wavered from her. As he approached, she was able to see the finer details of his features. His skin had translucent quality as if what you were seeing was steam beneath the surface. His eyes were glistening pools of purple and when he smiled, you could see the small fangs.

"Hello little one" he said, his voice again soliciting a tingling feeling throughout her body. "What in the dimensions brought you to my realm?" He smiled dangerously close to the cage opening.

Opening her mouth, she began explaining. As she paced around the cage as she got angrier with every point, she made about how horrible Wendy was and how she wanted her dead. The bell noise was ringing more feverous and she ended on simply screaming.

"I see" the voice pulling her from her rage.

"Are you really so sure he...loves you Tinkerbell?" her name feels like is slides off his tongue.

Peter! She had to snap herself out of the fog that changed her emotions so completely.

"And you want to be big enough to kill Wendy?" he tapped his lips with his finger. She found herself wishing she were that finger.

"Are you sure about this little one?" He tilted his head to the side narrowing his eyes "This is something quite dangerous you ask. Fairies are meant to be small."

Folding her arms across her chest she looked at him with the most serious face she could muster and nodding her head to confirm. Thinking of Peter smiling and knowing in her heart loved her. The only thing in her way was her size, she was just too small. That is all Wendy had, she was bigger.

"Well Tinkerbell" he continued to use her full name. "I can grant this wish for you. However, as with anything in life, there is a price."

Unfolding her arms and nodding her head towards him she assumed this magnificent creature, who could make Peter hers, would know she was determined no matter the cost.

"My name is Astaroth. It is my pleasure to meet you little one." With a gesture the cage disappeared. Tink was not sure how she knew this, she simply did. Flying up so she was level with his face she saw that he was smiling again. He turned and said "follow me" making his way back to the table where Imp had just been.

As they approached, she saw there were all manner of jars and bowls. There was also a tremendous amount of blood she had not seen before. Tink scanned the table she saw that there was a creature she didn't recognize, but his insides were on display and there was a terrible smell. She covered her mouth. Feeling nauseous, her stomach began to churn.

"I am a researcher little one. I find out all I can about creatures. For instance, I know that only fairies can hear what other fairies as saying. That to all other creatures it sounds like bells or chimes."

Warmth began to fill her the more words that came out of his mouth. Closing her eyes, careful not to take in a deep breath.

Pulling out a sheet of paper and then a feather, he dipped the quill it in a small bottle of a bluish colored liquid that had a little glitter. Tink flew in closer to see what it was.

"It is the blood of a fairy" he stated plainly.

Tink recoiled. Fear began to spread and before it could take hold completely, he said "Do not worry little one, I have to bind the spell in blood and a fairy" gesturing to the little bottle, "and this little one got trapped by a Molearth. The creature with the tentacles and jaws that almost had you before I found you. So, I made sure that her death was not in vain".

Tink wondered how many fairies had come to this place. "Not many" and he winked at her. Most do not have ambitions such as yours. Looking down again, she watched as he wrote. She knew she could not read the languages of other creatures and fairies did not have a written language.

"Alright. Are you ready?" Astaroth opened his hand and placed something on his palm. Tink flew down closer see what it is. It was three symbols on a piece of what looked like fabric which was about the length of one of her arms. Landing next to it she looked up at him questioning.

"All you need to do is pick it up and wrap it around yourself. Then you will become the size of Wendy. You will be the perfect size for your Peter." This made Tink incredibly happy. She held up the fabric and in touching it felt more like leather but thinner.

"It is skin" He stated. Feeling so happy that this was actually happening that the words didn't even register.

"I must tell you the terms of the deal Tinkerbell" his voice sounded more serious then before. "If you do this, you will be bound to serve me after Peter's death." Tink met his gaze, anger welling inside her. "Peter is a human. Their lives are fragile. You will have the length of his life with him, but after, you must return to me and serve me for a lifetime equal to mine." He waited for his words to sink in.

"Do we have a deal?" he asked.

Tink nodded. Removing her green fabric wrap, she then picked the skin up again and wrapped it around herself.

At first it was just cool against her skin. When the markings began glow and they dug into her skin, the pain was blinding. She tried to pull it off but that made it worse. Never having felt so much pain at the same time she eventually she blacked out for a second time today.

Slowly she opened her eyes.

She was laying on something rough, she sat up and looked around. Everything was smaller. Much smaller than she remembered it.

Looking down at her hands and then her legs. She was wearing pants of some kind. This was new as fairies never wore pants, or anything for that matter. Starting to stand she heard "Be careful, you are not used to the amount of room you will take up" when she looked to where the voice was coming from. He was sitting on a chair near her smiling. Not the same smile she realized; this one was with pride.

Standing up and reached out his hand to her. Taking it, she allowed him to pull her till she was standing. At first, she was unsteady and began to fall, and his arms went around to her catch her. When this happened, she was flooded with sensations she had never had before. Never having been held, except sitting in the palm of Peter's hand. She looked up into Astaroth face. His expression was caring, he wanted to help her. Sighing she began to imagine staying here with him, she was content.

As if sensing her thoughts, he said "What about Peter?" That snapped her thoughts back to Peter, she wondered how long she had been gone from him? Standing up releasing herself from Astaroth, because she could not focus when he was close, or talking.

She needed to get back to Peter.

Looking around she tried to find the door so she could make her way out. Astaroth smiled and walked up to her. "You just have to fly" he said pointing up "Do you remember how to do that little one?"

Nodding her head, she then closed her eyes. The thought of herself sitting next to Peter on the bed laughing the way he did with Wendy Imagining him tucking her hair behind her ear. She felt the air around her move and when she opened her eyes to find the designs on her body glowing blue and wings had changed from fairy wings to ones like a bat.

She spun around trying to get a better look but before she made herself dizzy, "You need wings big enough to carry you. Those will do. Astaroth winked and finished "Do not forget our bargain. When Peter's life is over you owe me a lifetime."

Launching into the air she felt a little bit of resistance. There was pressure, but happiness filled her heart. She was finally big enough to capture Peter's heart.

Racing through the stars she arrived to the window of the Darling house

The windows were dark but using the moonlight she peered inside The beds were empty. Where were they? Tink landed on the roof with a thump that surprised even her. Pacing back and forth she concentrated If she became confused sometimes it would take her hours to become unconfused. Then it hit her, Neverland!

Launching herself up again, raced through the sky, past the second star on the right and headed into the horizon as the morning sun was beginning to come up.

Spotting the camp for the Lost Boys beneath her, she looked around There was no activity which told Tink they were still asleep. She flew around and peeked in into the shelters until she saw Michael, he was cuddling his teddy bear with his brother John both in a hammock sound asleep.

There was a hammock next to them with a blanket but no Wendy Her eyes narrowed and she took off towards the top of the tree, where Peter lived.

Wendy had better not be there. Tink was the only person to ever sleep in Peter's room.

The happiness she had held in her heart on her way from the cave had vanished. She felt the heat rise and the marks on her body began to glow When she peered into the window, she saw Peter and Wendy laying on the mat he used for a bed. Her back to him, with his arm was around her with his head laying so close to hers they were almost touching.

Anger turned to rage.

She tried to fly into the window and slammed into the frame having forgotten her size. This made her even more angry. Now glowing super brightly as she slammed the door open and stormed in heading for the sleeping Wendy.

It was Peter who sat up with a start and his face turned to horror. What Tink saw was fear in his eyes. It was the same fear that she saw the first time he encountered Captain Hook. Did he believe she was dangerous?

"Peter" as she spoke the word seemed weird "Its me… Tink" he was still scrambling around "Your Tinkerbell…" her rage was sliding away into worry.

He finally grasped what he was looking for, his sword, he turned brandishing his sword and standing "What have you done with Tink?"

"Peter it is me… I'm bigger. The right size… for you" Her new voice wavering as she tried to move forward.

He slashed at the air in front of her "Stay back".

"Peter…" the word had barely left her lips when she heard a stifled scream and out of the corner of her eye she saw Wendy scramble from the mat to behind Peter.

"This is the last time I ask you Demon… WHAT…DID…YOU…DO…WITH… TINK!" his raised voice causing her to recoil. How did he now see it was her? How did he not know her? She looked up and saw his face which was a mixture of terror and anger. Behind him stood Wendy. He was protecting WENDY! She must have used some magic on Peter while Tink had been gone.

Fury coursed through her again.

She could feel it warming her, the markings glowed again. Peter's face now wore a mask of pure terror and Wendy was simply sobbing behind him. WENDY!

Launching towards Wendy, Peter swung his sword slicing into Tink's arm causing her to spin and swing her arm back towards him. Peter flew across the room and hit the wall dropping his sword.

Tink swooped it and grabbed it. She advanced on Wendy who was cowering against the wall. She stabbed until Wendy stopped both screaming and moving. There was blood everywhere. Instead of being repulsed by this, she felt victorious.

Then there was a gasp from behind her. Turning she saw it was Michael who was also crying, John who was staring in shock. Scanning further she noticed that the Lost Boys were also there and had their weapons. They were the doorway and at the windows some with bows aimed right at her.

Pockets, one of the smaller boys moved in towards Peter. He never took his eyes of her until he got to Peter and shook him "Peter" his voice nothing but a whisper.

Peter didn't move.

Tink started to move towards Peter, had hurt him? She never wanted to hurt Peter.

Before she reached him, she felt the piercing of two arrows into her back. Her friends were attacking her. They were stopping her from getting to Peter. Stopping her from helping him.

Another set of arrows were loosed. This time she heard them and moved before they could impact into her.

Turning to look into their eyes, her pain diminished, and her fury grew. Her anger was so intense she began to see spots of until her vision was only red in a blinding rage!

She was not sure how much time past when her vision began to clear. Looking down she was covered in a sticky wetness. Scanning her surroundings there were blood and bodies everywhere.

She looks over to where Peter had been to find him with his chest ripped open and his heart gone.

"Looking for this?"

Turning she saw Astaroth leaning against the far wall, he was holding a bloody heart in his hand. Tink moved towards him. She found herself wanting to feel mad that she found Wendy here, wanting to feel sorrowful that she had taken the life of Michael and John. Trying to feel mournful that she slain every Lost Boy and most of all she wanted to feel heartbroken that she lost her precious Peter. However, a strange realization settled over her.

It was that she now felt nothing at all.

"I put them all in here" gesturing with the heart. "They simply get in the way. Feelings." He shrugged "You can keep this where you would like Little One. It is yours." Holding the heart out to her.

Slowly walking over, she took it from him. She turned it over in her hands. Such a frail thing. Pulling a piece of fabric off on of the bodies, she wrapped it up.

"Are you ready?" he said smiling.

She nodded.

He reached out his hand scanning the room one final time "Dreams do come true, if only we wish hard enough" he met her gaze then "You can have anything in life if you will sacrifice everything else for it."

ERIKA LANCE

Erika had the unique opportunity to live in several different environments across the country growing up, giving her a colorful perspective on life. Born in Minnesota, she spent most of her formative years in Hollywood, then a ranch in New Mexico on the border of an Indian reservation. With a love of the arts since she was a child (acting, painting, sewing and dancing to name a few!) she found her passion in writing. Beginning with short stories, poems and articles for local papers. Remember, not every story has a happy ending.

www.erikalance.com

Twitter: AuthorELance

FaceBook: www.facebook.com/pages/authorelance

Instagram: AuthorELance

FAUST
FAUST

Carlton Herzog

Call me old-fashioned, but I likes my demons the way I likes my women: hot and nasty or what's the point of invoking them. I've come to associate a high standard of service with certain incidentals of the brand, such as the cloven hooves and curly horns, in much the same way car aficionados do with the Chrysler logo. To me, the reek of burning sulfur emanating from a portal is as sweet as the smell of cinnamon bread to a child standing outside a bakery.

So, you can well imagine my horror when my summoning spell conjured Good Jelly, a buck-toothed sausage fingered purple cousin of the Kool-Aid guy, and Little Evil, a lisping baby who skittered around on eight spider legs.

But the indignities did not end there.

Where there ought to have been any number of demonic symbols scrawled in blood, and a fog of sulfur choking the air, there were calm discussions of the pros and cons of free will accompanied by pipe smoke and Earl Grey tea.

That's not the worst of it. There's the trans-dimensional leakage where any and all paradoxes can gain a purchase in this world, not the least of which is that the demons overlap and pass through one another. Time runs backward while gravity comes and goes. It's enough to make a monkey crazy.

There are of course other problems that arise from diabolical co-associations, not the least of which is that Good Jelly and Little Evil like it here, so much so they have refused to leave, and have invited their friends to join them here on the earthly plane—in loathsome profusion.

Mind you I am as progressive as the next person. But nesting does create some unique problems for me. First, I can't have social life. How do you explain a small army of goofy looking demons carrying on like a bunch of frat boys? And then there's that whole miraculous multiplication thing. Think Jesus feeding the five thousand only instead of 1 piece of bread becoming many you have two demons increasing geometrically into a currently uncountable number. Because they are not restricted by our considerations of time and space, and little things like the Pauli exclusion principle, a thousand or more can all stand in one spot at the same time. Or sit, usually in my best recliner. My primate brain isn't cut out for the nuanced and granular perception of such a dynamic shifting reality unless it's heavily medicated. Thank God for Jack Daniels and blunts—two things that moron God got right.

The worst part is that they are increasing their numbers every day. So, when I asked Little Evil what they intended to do with all that demon power, he told me that they intended to retake and repurpose Hell so they can be redeemed.

So, I asked, "What do you mean repurpose?"

At that Good Jelly chimed in and said, "Hell began as a place of exile and incarceration for the losing side in a poly-dimensional territorial dispute. Once we're free, we can find a better use for it. I'm on the steering committee."

So, I said, "What about the damned?"

Little Evil said, "They don't exist; they never did. Nobody including God himself, knows if anything survives the death of a mortal body, and frankly nobody cares. Contrary to what you've been taught, humans are not the center of anything. Look around: 200 billion galaxies, each filled with 200 billion stars, and each star with its own set of planets. And that's just one bubble universe in one dimension. You can't get more insignificant than that. And yet you labor under the misguided belief that two super beings have nothing better do than battle for the souls of man."

I said, "We mortals cling to anything that gives us hope. Our positive illusions keep us going, however silly they seem to you."

Little Evil said, "Not silly. Just counterproductive. You waste a lot of time, energy and treasure blaming the Devil for your problems, on the one hand, while waiting for God to come down and solve them, on the other. Your boy Einstein once observed that insanity is doing the same self-destructive thing over and over again expecting different results. Another way to see it is that you people don't learn, and more critically, you don't learn that you don't learn. I suspect that there's a cognitive defect at work here that evolution may or may not correct. Only time will tell. You, Sir, won't be around to see that blessed day should it occur, but, if it's any consolation, we will."

When Good Jelly and Little Evil expounded on their redemption plan and just how stupid we humans are I felt like Dorothy when she pulled ~~~~~~~~~~~~~~~ that the Great and Powerful Oz was only a man. Or when ~~~~~~ more like a drunk uncle on ski~~~~~~~~~~~~~~~~~~ global supe power.

One day as I was dodging demonic vapors, Good Jelly asked me if wanted to pay a visit to Hell.

He said, "not permanently, but a quick in and out look at what waiting for you."

I said, "sure, what could it hurt."

Then he stabbed me in the forehead with a large kitchen knife. For moment, wasn't sure what had happened. But after my head cleared knew that I was dead. Since I had renounced shrooms and acid long ago how else could I explain hovering above my motionless blood-smeared body? My ethereal musings were interrupted by a powerful gust of wind carrying me up through the ceiling and into a large tear in the sky. Sta flashed past me in streaks of colored light until I alighted in a hotel lobb

The next thing I knew I was standing before the façade of an enor mous hotel. On the lawn behind me a sign read WELCOME TO ETERNIT in big bold flaming red letters. It was flanked by two enormous pitchfor wielding devils. I entered and went up to the hostess. She had the re dest lips and palest skin I had ever seen on woman. She wore a red blous and a black leather skirt with a slit in the back for her serpentine tail. He nametag read Maltista, Head Succubus.

"Mr. Faust, I presume."

"Yes."

"Welcome to Eternity. May I see your Visa?"

Somehow, I knew what she meant. I reached into my now blood free shirt and retrieved the document in question.

"From your paperwork, I see that your stay in Hell will be temporar You have your choice of room, suite, cottage or tent."

"I'll take a room."

"Excellent choice. Remember this is family run hotel where you'll fin demonic hospitality with a human touch. Do you want me to have th concierge take your bags up?"

I hadn't noticed the bags before and gave her a quizzical look.

"Those are your so-called sins Mr. Faust. The big suitcase is for the mortal ones; the little one is for peccadillos and misdemeanors. Bongo Jerry is our concierge. He'll bring them up for you."

Bongo Jerry was a raptor in an admiral's uniform. The astonished look on my face prompted Maltista to remark: "He's a big fan of Jurassic Park

I said, "Wait a minute. What about the fire and brimstone, the demons torturing the damned with pitchforks and rivers of fire?"

"We have all manner of Hospitality packages for our guests. What you have described is just one of our many kink packages. You can order that if you like. We also have the landscape of open graves with a mass of twisted and emaciated corpses trying to eat you. Or you can swim around in a river of boiling blood along with other bodies and be poked and prodded by a regiment of centaurs. Or we can fuse your body to a dead tree in the wood of the damned, and let you get pecked by Harpies. It's all up to you Mr. Faust."

"So what Good Jelly told me is true: Hell isn't a place of punishment, shame, moral condemnation."

"Nope. That's a tall tale we have spread to keep folks from offing themselves every time the going gets rough up there. It's just a relaxed waiting room for the soul."

"Where is it exactly?"

"Think of the universe as a great ball. Hell is its circumference or bound. Hence the name, the Hotel at the End of The Universe. You can tour the circle by rail if you like, see all the sights from above. Rent a pet to keep you company or purchase one or more escorts."

"Would that take a very long time?"

"We can manipulate the perception of time here, so a million years seems like a day, or a day seems lie a million years, So, an extended train ride for a million years could be said to seem only as long as one from Milan to Paris. Why, look—it's our house comedian Diabolicus. Hey D, got a joke for our new guest?"

D laughed and said, "I sure do. Guy dies and goes to heaven. When he gets to the Pearly Gates, Saint Peter says you're too much of a sinner for this place."

The guy says, 'That's nonsense. How many times did I take the Lord's name in vein?'

Saint Peter says, 'A million six.

The guys says, 'a million six! Jesus Christ that's a lot!'

We all laughed at the blasphemous humor.

"Thank you for helping Mr. Faust feel welcome D. Now off with you. Mr. Faust, what kind of food do you like?"

"I'm dead, why do I need food at all?"

"Many of our guests still like to enjoy a good meal. Your hospitality package could be coded for normal human appetites and nutrition requirements. You have the option of a room with a kitchenette and grocery delivery, room service, or simply visit the banquet room which serves 24 hours a day seven days a week. The only thing not on the menu is other people. Some things are not permitted and encouraging cannibalism is one of them."

"Fine."

As I stood there. Elvis and Buddy Holly came strolling by in route to the banquet hall. They were laughing and joking.

I said, "I get why Elvis is here, but not Buddy Holly."

She said, "Buddy would wake up every morning and shoot God the double-bird and say, 'You sir, are a piece of shit. Of course, such blasphemy counts for nothing in the long run, since there is no actual punishment for sins just a weak acknowledgment.'

I said, "Good to know. I'll freshen up and then go have a few drinks."

After Maltista finished my paperwork, she said "Bongo Jerry will take your bags. After he took me to the room, I searched in my pockets for a tip but there was neither change nor bills.

He saw what I was about and hissed, "No need Sir. The pleasure is all mine. Besides, here the only coin of the realm is goodwill."

After I cleaned up, I headed over to the Bizarro Lounge. The sign over the vestibule read ANYTHING GOES!

As I walked over to the large circular bar, I noticed that there was a peculiar division of labor. Babies smelling of talc and shampoo walked or crawled along the bar taking drink orders then in gurgling tones called them out to headless pourers in black ties and vests.

Incredulous, I just stared. One of the babies saw me and drooled as babies are wont to do. It slithered over and asked me in the underdeveloped palette lisp of a toddler what I was drinking. Maintaining my composure, I replied "Jack Daniels. Make it a double."

In the next moment, I was, drink in hand, standing at the edge of a sunlit field filled with apple trees. Yards away I could see a man and a woman naked except for fig leaves covering their privates. They were diligently picking apples and tossing them into a massive juicer. They were watched by a coiled cobra that hissed at them to "Work faster; money doesn't grow on trees." A few feet away an old man worked in a flower garden. He wore a white toga and sandals. He had majestic white hair and beard together with a stern disapproving face. He wore Mr. Magoo thick glasses. He was angry about their theft of apples. He then yelled the man and the woman to "Get out before I throw you out." When the did the man and the woman stopped picking apples, walked over to his flower bed and urinated. The cobra laughed and then hissed "Shame on you. That's no way to treat your father."

Then I heard applause and was seated back in the bar. Apparently, the Bizarro hospitality package included an impromptu and snarky take on the Fall of Man. It was followed by Diabolicus' short comedy routine called The Three Doors.

Guy dies and goes to hell. Devil says you can pick your punishment from what's behind these three doors. He opens the first door, and everybody is standing on their head atop a wooden floor. He shakes his head and says, 'No way.'

He opens the second door, and the scenario is the same except the floor is made of concrete. He closes the door and says, 'what else do you have?'

The Devil points to the third door. The guy opens it, and everyone is standing in shit up to their knees, but are otherwise drinking coffee, smoking cigarettes. Naturally, the guy picks the third door. He walks in, closes the door behind himself, grabs a cup of coffee and chats up a buxom redhead.

A moment later the Devil reopens the third door, sticks his head in and yells, "Okay--coffee break's over; everybody back on your head."

Hysterical. I had a few more drinks and left. As I walked back to my room, I thought ain't Hell grand? It has the worst P.R. but the best hospitality. I wouldn't mind sticking around here for all eternity.

When I passed through the lobby, I stopped to thank the hostess for the good time I was having. Maltista was gone. In her place was her sister Malvista.

I said, "this is the best hotel I have ever stayed at."

She smiled and said, "Of course it is. It has all the bells and whistles and you've only seen but a few. I can show you more if you like. But there is a catch."

"Tell me."

"Well, you're short timer. That means you don't have enough time to see much more. You would have to sign a waiver of relief. A small formality."

"Is this a trick?"

"Heavens no. But even if it were, you said yourself hell is a great place to spend eternity, so what's the big deal."

I didn't think they had to trick me into anything, since I was already in hell and at their mercy. So, I signed the waiver. And ⸻ ⸻ red on her promise. I had an amazing time. When it was over, I expected to be whisked back to the land of the living.

But she said, "you should have read the fine print. You permanently waived your right of return. Your fate is now in the discretion of the presiding authority, namely, Lucifer. He, always magnanimous, has decided to be merciful."

I thought for a moment then said, "So I won't be baked or broiled for all time?"

"That would be barbaric."

"So, what are you going to do to me?"

"You get the Third Door."

"And with that she snapped her fingers, and the next thing I knew I was standing in this shit pile with you losers. How long do these breaks last?"

THE END

CARLTON HERZOG

I always feel uncomfortable with self-description given my natural tendency toward puffery. What I can say is that I am a veteran of the United States Air Force (flight dispatcher). Thanks to Uncle Sam, I was able to live all over the world and acquire the GI. Bill. The latter paid for some of my education (Rutgers, B.A. magna cum laude; J.D. Rutgers Law and Articles Editor of the Rutgers Law Review).

As an author, I do not confine myself to any genre. If something interests me, then I try it. I have published two law review articles that have been commended in the National Law Journal. My writing reflects an uncompromising social awareness and responsibility. I am more concerned with ideas than character development. Overall, my writing is peppered unflattering assessments of carnivores, climate change deniers, gun-owners, polluters, racists, and religious hypocrites.

As a reader, I like books that have something meaningful to say about the human condition, and those tend to be non-fiction. I may move in fictional worlds, but I live in the real one. My guilty pleasures belong to my love for lifting weights as well as painting and sculpting. My art has graced the cover of Schlock Webzine. I also use it as my personal emblem since it is far more compelling than my face.

amazon.com/author/carltonherzog

notapipepublishing.com

BROM BONES RIDES AGAIN
LEGEND OF SLEEPY HOLLOW

Valerie Puri

CHAPTER 1

"Cheers," I raise my pint, tapping it against the other's glasses. The gang and I get together every year to catch up on old times. We grew up with each other in Vermont, but all went our separate ways after college. This sleepy town in New York was a spot where the three of us could meet in the middle and unwind.

Lightning flashes outside the old pub in Mount Pleasant. Large rain droplets start pelting the rippled panes of glass. Headlights from the occasional car driving by cast long shadows inside the dim bar. I like how the place has looked the same for nearly two hundred years, right down to the hand-dipped candles on the tables.

After taking a deep gulp of beer, I set my glass on the rustic table.

"You know," I say, wiping the foam from my mustache with a napkin. "There's an old legend in these parts."

"Sure, Jack, we've all heard of the legend of sleepy hollow," Peter snorts.

"Mmhmm," Chester agrees as he takes another drink.

"You haven't heard the real legend," I pull the candle closer to me and lean over it so the light will cast shadows on my face. "It happened a long time ago on a stormy night just like this...."

Thunder rumbled as Abraham 'Brom Bones' Van Brunt approached the Van Tassel's stately manor. Candlelight blazed from every window on that autumn evening. A fiddler's merry tune teased the night air with the merriment happening inside.

Only those of importance were invited to the Van Tassel's harvest party. The growing season had been successful and a cornucopia of delights was ready for Tarrytown to enjoy through the winter months. But first, the Van Tassels, Van Brunts, and other esteemed members of society would enjoy the first taste of the autumn crop.

Brom dismounted his horse at the front stoop of the manor. He took a small pinch of salt from his saddlebag and let the horse lick it from his hand.

"We have to keep you nice and strong, Cannon." He said, patting the horse's neck.

A stable hand rushed up to take the reins.

"Brush him down, but keep him saddled," Brom instructed. "I may need to leave at a moment's notice. Mind not to touch the saddle bags, I don't want my cargo disturbed."

"Yes, sir," the boy, no older than twelve, said. He ushered Cannon to the stables.

Brom cleared his throat and adjusted his waistcoat before going in.

A servant opened the door for him and the warm manor welcomed him with open arms.

"Brom Bones!" Baltus Van Tassel called from across the room at his entrance.

Brom stood tall and strode over to his future father-in-law. Tonight, he would ask for Katrina's hand in marriage. The union of their two prestigious families would ensure Tarrytown would prosper for generations to come.

"Mr. Van Tassel," Brom gave a half-bow to show respect. "What a wonderful evening party you have thrown. This is a night people will remember for years."

"You flatter me, Brom, as you know I..."

Baltus continued talking, but Brom tuned him out. He spotted a troubling scene from the far side of the room. His soon-to-be betrothed was engaged in a conversation with that lanky schoolmaster, Ichabod Crane.

The very sight of it made Brom's face burn hot.

The schoolmaster was new to Tarrytown, but the people welcomed him warmly. Everyone except Brom. He saw Ichabod for who he was: a coward and a threat to Brom's marriage plans.

Brom Bones Rides Again by Valerie Puri

Katrina, being the well brought up lady that she was, was too polite to tell Ichabod he needed to excuse himself from her company.

Every time Ichabod was in the same room as Katrina, he always drifted near her. If Brom didn't know any better, he would say the schoolmaster was after more than just gentile conversation.

Brom narrowed his eyes. Ichabod was pursuing his future bride. It was time to put a stop to it.

"Therefore, with the war over and our new republic firmly established, prosperity is there for those who dare to acquire it," Baltus stated proudly.

"My dear, sir, I must beg your pardon," Brom said with another slight bow. "I see your dear daughter Katrina and I must give my regards to her. I fear it would be rude not to."

"Of course, dear boy," Baltus laughed heartily, his round belly jostling as he chuckled. "The moon is not yet high, there will be plenty of time to discuss business after the pleasantries are dispensed. Although with these storms, I doubt we'll see even the stars tonight."

Brom navigated his way through the parlor, eager to intervene on the improper courtship Ichabod was attempting.

"The best way to learn something is by partaking in the activity itself. I always encourage my students to—"

Brom had to free Katrina from whatever nonsense Ichabod was droning on about. He took it upon himself to swoop in and save her from a one-sided conversation.

"Katrina, you look radiant." Brom took her gloved hand, kissing it lightly. Her pink, pouty lips curved into a smile. Brom was eager to kiss those lips on the day of their wedding.

She curtsied, her lavender gown puddling delicately on the floor as she dipped down.

"Mr. Van Brunt."

"Please, my dear, call me Brom. We are destined for more than such formalities, you and I."

Katrina blushed as her eyelashes fluttered coyly.

Ichabod's face also turned red, but not from embarrassment. Brom puffed out his muscular chest and acknowledged the schoolmaster.

"Mr. Crane, how good of you to join the festivities." Quite frankly, Brom was surprised that such a lowly commoner was even invited.

"It's a pleasure to be here in the company of these fine folks," the scrawny man said.

"Come," Brom clasped his large hand on Ichabod's bony shoulder, "let's partake of the bounty this feast has to offer."

He ushered Ichabod away from Katrina with a courteous nod in her direction. What a fool he was to think he had a chance with his betrothed.

"How is that horse of yours? What's the steed's name again?"

"G-gunpowder," Ichabod squeaked.

"Gunpowder, that's it," Brom boomed in his commanding voice. "You need a horse with a strong name. Take my stallion, Cannon, for example. He's stronger than a bull and twice as large. He has a coat so black that it takes on a blue shimmer when the light hits it just right. A horse that magnificent deserves a powerful name. Wouldn't you agree?"

"Why yes, as you say, Brom."

"You can call me Mr. Van Brunt, if you please," Brom grinned. "You see, just like horses, even men need strong names, eh, Ichabod?"

The schoolmaster screwed up his face in confusion.

Brom took a pair of glasses from a nearby sideboard. He filled them up with a fine brandy and gave one to Ichabod. He took the offered drink with boney fingers.

"A toast to new friendship."

They clanked their glasses together and tipped the contents down their throats. The liquid went down smooth for Brom.

Ichabod took one sip and started coughing and wheezing.

Brom chortled. "Soon you'll be able to drink that like a real man, Ichabod. How about some eggs to settle your stomach?"

He placed a pickled egg on a small plate. To help bring out the vinegar brine, he sprinkled a heavy dusting of salt on top.

"Try this delectable treat," he offered the plate to Ichabod.

The schoolmaster's oversized nose crinkled when he smelled it. Gingerly, he lifted the fork and took a small bite.

"Ack," Ichabod spat. "That's quite...bitter."

"The more bitter the better when it comes to pickled eggs! Is that not the case where you're from, Mr. Crane?"

Ichabod dabbed at his mouth with his handkerchief. "If I may say so, the eggs are not so poignant back home."

As the night wore on, Brom continued to play his pranks on Ichabod Crane. The schoolmaster continued to grow increasingly flummoxed while Brom grew more confident. No one in the room even suspected that helpful Brom was the source of Ichabod's frustration. Not even Katrina.

Soon, Ichabod would reveal himself as unworthy to even be in the same room as her.

"Ichabod, you're new to our beloved Tarrytown," Brom announced so the room could hear. "You, being a schoolmaster, must enjoy stories and tales of intrigue. Have you ever heard the haunting tales of Sleepy Hollow?"

Ichabod's lower lip trembled. "Hauntings in Sleepy Hollow? Surely you don't mean the Sleepy Hollow where my quarters are?"

"Certainly, I do. You should be especially interested to hear the tale then!"

"My dear boy Brom, are you going to regale us with a story?" Mr. Van Tassel asked excitedly.

"It would be my pleasure, sir."

Brom gripped Ichabod by the shoulder and lead him over to the grand fireplace. He pushed Ichabod into an oversized chair, making the scrawny man look even smaller.

Katrina glided across the floor and sat in a dainty chair, her blue eyes eager to hear the tale.

This was the moment Brom Bones Van Brunt had been waiting for. Nothing revealed a coward like a ghost story.

CHAPTER 2

Brom settled into a chair with his back to the fireplace, casting his face in deep shadows. Thunder rumbled outside the manor. Soon, rain pattered against the windows.

It was the perfect backdrop for a frightful tale.

Brom surveyed his audience. Baltus sat eagerly in his seat, ready to be entertained. Ichabod shrank into the cushions of the wingback chair. Katrina was poised, delicate as a flower, her auburn curls reflecting the firelight. Others gathered round, ready for a good rendition of the local legends they knew so well.

"As you travel just down the road, be careful, for there lies the restless spirit of Major Andre," Brom began. "A spy planted in the Continental Army by the British, Major Andre conspired with the traitor Benedict Arnold. For his treason, he was hung by the neck from the large tulip tree at the bend in the road."

Brom gripped his hand around his throat as if demonstrating a hanged man. Ichabod took a deep gulp from his tankard of ale. A smile tugged at

Brom's lips to see the schoolmaster so nervous. He was only getting started.

"Be warned, any man who passes by that spot is in danger! The ghost of Major Andre roams the area seeking his British counterparts. He attacks any American who treads on his land at night," Brom lunged forward at Ichabod, causing him to start and slosh his ale. "The Major never stops seeking revenge on the Yankees who ended his life before he could finish his mission."

Ichabod swallowed audibly.

"The traitor deserved what he got," Baltus Van Tassel harrumphed.

"Father, his spirit still terrorizes us," Katrina added in her angelic voice. She tugged at the fingertips of her gloves. "We should be mindful of the dead. Maybe then he will leave us in peace."

"Superstition and folly," Baltus boomed, dismissing his daughter's words.

"What do you think, Ichabod?" Brom asked. "Do you believe in such superstitions?"

Ichabod hid behind his tankard, nodding.

"I always c-carry a little salt with me, to ward off s-spirits," the schoolmaster stuttered nervously.

Brom laughed.

"Ah, but there are more terrors in this land aside from Major Andre's enraged spirit. You'll need more than just a little bit of salt, for what comes next." Brom sneered. "As you venture through the wooded swamp back to Sleepy Hollow, pray you do not come upon the dreaded headless horseman."

For dramatic effect, he paused to drink from his own tankard. He took a moment to study Katrina. His love was fixated on him with wide eyes. Eyes only for him. She didn't even glance in Ichabod's direction. His plan was working.

"The horseman is a long-forgotten soldier who lost his head to a cannonball during a terrible battle. Each night he rides on a horse black as midnight with eyes the fiery red of hell, searching for his missing head! The horseman is a frightfully large man, clad all in black. He wears a long cape that trails behind him as he rides...

"Many a rider has gone down that path never to be seen again. It is said that the Headless Horseman rode them down, decapitating them with his sword." Brom picked up a blunt butter knife and pantomimed slicing Ichabod's throat. "His blade cuts so finely the body continues on, unaware of it's missing crown, like a chicken picked for supper."

Katrina let out a whimper. Brom felt bad for frightening her with the graphic description, but one look at Ichabod's flushed face made it all worth while.

"Never able to replace his head with those of his victims, he has resorted to carrying a lit jack-o-lantern. Despite this, the Horseman never stops seeking a replacement head. If you look upon the flaming eyes of that carved pumpkin, it will be the last thing you ever see. If you come upon him, it could be your head next."

Brom held out his finger, panning the room with his outstretched hand. He stopped at Ichabod, pointing at him. The schoolmaster ducked his head down between his shoulders, trembling.

Fear hovered throughout the silent parlor.

"But there is hope!" Brom added with a lighter tone, causing Ichabod to perk up. "If you can cross the old covered bridge before the horseman you will be safe, for his demon horse cannot cross over."

"Hang on a minute," Chester interrupts. "This sounds like the same old legend. I thought you said this was different, Jack?"

I take another gulp of beer. "All in good time, guys. I'm getting to the good part."

The rain is still pelting the old pub, maintaining the spooky mood for the legend.

"Some say Brom made up the safe haven of the bridge to give Ichabod false hope. But others believed it to be true. Only those brave enough to test the legend really knew for sure."

Peter leans in. "So what happened next?"

CHAPTER 3

Ichabod was so unnerved he spent the rest of the evening huddled by the fire, cradling his tankard.

Katrina looked down upon him pityingly. She went to speak to him after Brom recounted the legend, but he jumped with a start, sloshing ale on her dress.

She hurried away, embarrassed of her spoiled gown, as Ichabod made a disheartened attempt to apologize.

Brom watched from the far side of the room. Ichabod's faux pas was the final nail in the coffin. Any chance he may have had with Katrina was gone.

Brom finished his ale and handed his empty cup to a servant. He approached Baltus with his head held high.

"Mr. Van Tassel," he said confidently. "As you know, our two families are vital to Tarrytown. We each hold a strong influential and financial position. Together, we can become even stronger." Brom added a respectful pause. "Sir, I would like to ask for Katrina's hand in marriage."

Baltus ran his hand up his chins and stroked his mutton chops, thinking.

"Young Brom Bones Van Brunt, I accept. I give you permission to marry my daughter."

Brom grinned. "Thank you, sir."

He turned to see the schoolmaster staring at him with his mouth hanging open. That one look said it all: Ichabod heard every word. He lost.

Brom was one step closer to having everything he ever wanted. He would make a good husband to Katrina. She would live a life of comfort and want for nothing.

Downtrodden, Ichabod left the party with his head hung low. A stable boy brought his horse to him. The schoolmaster put on his green tricorn hat and mounted Gunpowder.

At least the rain had stopped. The last thing Ichabod wanted was to ride home defeated, heartbroken, and in the middle of a rainstorm.

The clouds still covered the night sky, blocking out the moon. As he road away from the lively party in the well-lit Van Tassel manor, the darkness of night enveloped him.

Gunpowder lumbered along the road back to Sleepy Hollow. Katrina was the only woman who captured Ichabod's heart. He resolved to remain unwed to show his devotion to her. Perhaps there was a small chance she would refuse to marry Brom. With the tiniest hope still lingering, he decided he would remain in Tarrytown.

Lightning blazed through the sky, removing the dark shroud of night.

Ichabod looked up, startled at the sudden brightness. His breath caught when he saw where he was. At the bend in the road, the looming tulip tree stood. Its limbs stretched out like angry hands grabbing for him.

Gunpowder grew skittish around the tree. As the wind rustled the branches, a deep moaning crept from the edge of the woods. Ichabod recalled the tale of the traitor Major Andre.

"Yan-kee," a slow, deep voice called from the tree. "Yan-kee."

His stomach twisted in a knot as he shuddered. The vengeful ghost was there ready to attack him at any moment. He urged his horse forward, eager to leave the tulip tree behind.

Shortly after rounding the bend, Ichabod heard hooves trailing him. No one left the party at the same time as him, and the horse was matching his speed. Afraid it might be the angry spirit of Major Andre, he lowered his head, trying to hide behind the collar of his coat, and urged Gunpowder forward.

Thump, thump. Thump, thump.

The horse's hooves behind him increased in pace along with his heartbeat. He could not tell which was pounding louder in his head.

Gunpowder came to a stop at a crossroads. Ichabod squinted in the dark to try and find the right path. He wanted to get away from his pursuer, but he couldn't make out any landmarks letting him know which way to go.

He realized the rider behind him had also stopped...

Thinking maybe the rider was also just another lost person, he craned his head behind him to look.

A large figure in a black cloak was mounted on a massive horse, black as night. The tale of the headless horseman crept back into his mind. Ichabod was terrified.

He mustered his courage to offer help in case this really was another disoriented traveler.

"Hello stranger. Are you lost?" He called out to the mysterious rider.

There was no answer.

The horse lowered its head, revealing the rider held a lantern in his lap.

Ichabod squinted. The lantern's glow resembled a face. It had eyes, a nose, and a terrible grinning mouth. Drawing in a sharp gasp, he realized it wasn't a lantern at all. It was a jack-o-lantern. This was the headless horseman.

CHAPTER 4

Ichabod twisted back in his saddle to try and find his path. He had to get out of there, quickly. Another flash of lightning illuminated the sky, revealing the covered bridge in the distance.

Without hesitation, he spurred Gunpowder on, racing toward the bridge. The headless horseman was hot on his trail.

Faster and faster, Ichabod urged his steed forward. They were approaching the bridge. But so was the headless rider.

The clatter of his horse's hooves on the wood echoed inside the covered bridge. Ichabod was almost there. He could make it to safety if he just went a little further.

He reined in Gunpowder when he cleared the other side of the bridge. He had made it. He actually made it.

Looking back to make sure he really escaped, the headless rider's horse reared up in time with another flash of lightning. It pawed angrily at the air.

A deep hollow laugh erupted from the cavity between the horseman's shoulders. The menacing laugh sent chills up Ichabod's spine.

The horseman raised the jack-o-lantern over his neck where his head should have been. The image was horrific. A cursed rider with a flaming pumpkin head, mounted on a demon horse. With incredible strength, the headless horseman threw the carved pumpkin.

The jack-o-lantern nearly collided with Ichabod's face. It grazed his temple, knocking off his hat. The pumpkin smashed on the ground in a blaze of flames.

Spooked, Gunpowder sped off with Ichabod clinging desperately to his braided mane.

With the schoolmaster out of earshot, the headless horseman's deep laughter transformed into a hearty chortle. The rider removed his black cloak, balling it up and stuffing it into his saddle bag.

Brom Bones leaned forward to pat Cannon on the neck.

"You did good, boy. We sure scared the wits out of Ichabod Crane."

He laughed so hard he had to wipe tears from his eyes. Never did he think his plan would work that well. The look on the schoolmaster's face was worth making up a lie to sneak out of the party early.

Brom laughed so loud, he didn't hear the hooves approaching him from behind. Nor did he hear the ring of steel as it was drawn from its sheath.

When he finally turned his horse around to go home, his laughter caught in his throat.

Before him was the real headless horseman in all his unholy glory.

The horse was so black, it nearly disappeared into the night...except for its glowing, red eyes. It snorted angrily, steam from the fires of hell escaping its nostrils. The horseman raised his arm, letting his cape freely flap in the wind. He surged forward, swinging down his raised arm.

Brom ducked as a flash of metal whipped through the air. The sword came so close to his head he could hear it whistle as it sped past his ear.

The headless horseman raised his arm again, preparing for another attack.

Knowing the bridge was just behind him, Brom turned Cannon sharply around.

"Heeyah!"

He kicked Cannon's flank, and the trusty steed bolted onto the covered bridge. His relief turned to terror as he heard a second set of hooves pounding on the wooden planks.

The stories were wrong. The bridge wasn't a haven.

Brom reached the other side and dared to glance back. The demon horse with its blazing red eyes and its headless rider were barreling over the bridge. The horse was faster than any Brom had ever known. Only a mount from hell could possess such speed...

"Faster, Cannon, faster," Brom urged as they galloped through the darkness.

The headless horseman was gaining on him. Soon, the demon horse was riding just beside him.

Thinking fast for something, anything, Brom reached into his saddle bag and grabbed a fistful of salt. He usually gave a little of the salt to Cannon in his grain or as a treat so he would stay strong and healthy.

Earlier in the evening, he had laughed at Ichabod for using salt to ward off spirits. Now the mineral was all he had to save himself.

He threw the salt at the headless rider, but not before the horseman swung his sword one final time at Brom's neck.

When the salt made contact, the demon horse and rider vaporized into a cloud of purple smoke. Brom and his horse rode through the haze. His hands still gripped the reins as Cannon galloped away into the night, leaving Brom's head in the swamp behind them...

Chapter 5

"When Brom threw the salt at the headless horseman, he banished the spirit's physical form, but not the spirit itself. That cloud of purple smoke took hold of Cannon and Brom, and the headless horseman had a new body. To this day, Brom Bones rides again on the same night each year— this night—searching for his head in the swamp by the old bride."

Chester and Peter stare at me with wide eyes. I tip the dredges of beer at the bottom of my glass into my mouth. It doesn't taste as good now that it's warm, but I swallow and bear it.

"What ever happened to Ichabod?" Peter asks.

"He was never seen in Tarrytown again. Some say he died, that the horseman got him. The next morning Katrina found the smashed pumpkin next to Ichabod's green hat. They even say she found Brom's head and buried it at the side of the road. Grieving the loss of her two suitors, she wore black from that day on, mourning the married life she never had."

"Woah," Chester looks pale. "That's heavy stuff."

We order some food and spend the next couple hours catching up on what's happening in our lives. I yawn, tired from staying up so late.

"I'm going to head back to my hotel. Good night guys, see you tomorrow."

I leave the pub, glad the rain has finally stopped. Gravel crunches under my feet as I walk to my car. The night air is calm. The rain must have drove all the animals into hiding—not even the crickets are out. I shudder at how quiet it is.

After starting my car, I put it into gear. I nursed the same beer all night, so I was sober enough to drive back.

As I head to the hotel, I decide to take a detour. I want to pay homage to old Ichabod Crane and Brom Van Brunt.

After I park my car, I get out and walk to the edge of the old covered bridge. It's amazing the thing is still here. I gingerly step onto the old wooden planks. The air feels charged, like static electricity is all around me.

Curious if the tale I told is really true, I walk across the bridge to the other side. This is where Brom must have seen the real headless horseman.

A plume of purple smoke materializes in front of me. I stumble backwards, startled.

A black horse with a rider steps out from the purple tendrils. The horse's eyes flicker like red flames. In the moonlight, I can see the rider has no head. He grabs something at his hip with a black-gloved hand. The sharp steel sings as he draws his sword from the sheath.

"Holy hell!"

I scramble across the bridge and fling my car door open. Thank God I left the keys in the ignition, because fumbling with them right now was the last thing I wanted to do.

Without thinking, I start the car and slam my foot on the gas.

As I put distance between myself and the old bridge, I glance in the rear-view mirror. The headless horseman and his demon horse are chasing me. Thankfully, they can't keep up with my car, and they soon disappear from view.

"Well I'll be damned. Brom Bones rides again."

THE END

VALERIE PURI

Valerie Puri is an author of Paranormal, Fantasy, and Young Adult. As an author of both short stories and novels, she enjoys the flexibility of writing tales of any length. Her favorite aspect of writing is the ability to create something out of nothing. She loves building worlds readers can visualize and filling those worlds with complex characters and storylines. Valerie believes that the experiences we have in life are just stories waiting to be written.

In 2016, she published her debut novel, The Crimson Tree, a thrilling paranormal tale inspired by true events. The main source of inspiration for this story was a number of experiences her sister encountered in her home. She went on to publish The Dociles, book one of The Secret Archives Trilogy, her young adult dystopian series. Valerie's work can be found in anthologies such as Demonic Anthologies, Thrill of the Hunt, and Once Upon Academy. Readers can look forward to future novels and short stories with paranormal and urban fantasy aspects in the near future.

When she's not writing, she enjoys spending time with her family, traveling, or listening to audio books. She is a Florida transplant, but part of her will always call the Midwest home.

Connect with Valerie

Facebook: @AuthorValeriePuri

Facebook Group: www.facebook.com/groups/puripals

Instagram: @AuthorValeriePuri

Twitter: @ValeriePuri

BookBub: www.bookbub.com/authors/valerie-puri

Website: www.valeriepuri.com

Newsletter: www.valeriepuri.com/contact

REMEMBER LENORE
THE RAVEN

Jessica Chaleff

Chimes of midnight rang throughout the seaside abode, rustling awake the man who dwelled within. Peeling his cheek from the page of a book he had fallen asleep whilst reading, the man lifted his head, to briefly in his stupor, check his surroundings. His desk had become more of a welcome place to slumber than his bedroom, cold from misuse, and frozen in time. Remaining in his state of twilight, a tapping at his front door caught his ear, and, quickly, sleep was an option no more.

"The wind," the man mumbled, "it was only the wind. Some loose pebbles hit my door... and nothing more."

It was another December. A lonely, dark December. This month no longer brought any source of merriness into his heart, not since the death of his wife, Lenore. Her disappearance had mystified many, as no one would confess to the crime, and nobody could be found, so here the man sits alone, pining for her more than ever on this lonely December night.

Her face was frozen in time on his desk, surrounded by an ornate frame, a constant reminder of her beauty, her warmth, her love. Those gorgeous orbs of blue, and hair, the fair brown of a woodland meadow, cheeks flushed rose, and lips full. The man looked upon the portrait as he has done many nights before, but no longer did it fill him with the warmth he so desired on these cold nights.

However, something was more unsettling upon this night, more than the coldness issuing from the portrait. He had felt his heart race from paranoia many nights before, but tonight was something fantastic. As his curtains rustled from an uncertain source, his heart lept from his chest, filling him with terror, his face turning paler than the pages of the book that lie prone before him.

"It must be the wind. No one is here." He gazed into the eyes of the portrait. "No one is ever here, not since Lenore. Just the wind, and nothing more."

The wind wasn't blowing as devilishly as the man convinced himself it to be, as it was barely strong enough to rustle a leaf, let alone spray errant pebbles at his door. There must be someone outside his home, lightly knocking, wanting entry, or perhaps a word. But at midnight? Nothing good could come from an unannounced visitor arriving at midnight. Gathering all the courage he could muster, the man, with feathery footsteps, approached the door and opened it wide, hoping the meet the source of the repeating sound... but there was no one. No source of the sound in sight. Nothing but the cold, isolating night. As he stood, ignoring the winter air making a meal of his aging bones, his ears shifted at a new sound, a whisper, wafting towards him. He swore, in his new clarity, the voice was saying: Lenore. Lenore. Lenore.

"Who's there?" His voice had found a false sense of courage and boomed into the night. "Who's there and why do you mention Lenore? Why must you remind me of Lenore?"

The night was silent. He may have found some clarity, but sleep was consuming him. That must be the answer. Truly, he is hearing things, and nothing more. As soon as the door closed behind him, the tapping was quick to resume. This is no hallucination brought on by the need for slumber. In a fit of rage, the man flung open the door, only to fall sharply on his backside, as a great shape, as black as the night, dove at him. He arched his head to peer at his desk and saw, a lone Raven, peering seemingly intrigued at the open book. Ignoring the pain from his tumble, he slowly closed the door, filled with not intrigue, but terror, at the sudden aviary visitor. A Raven flying into his home after midnight, what omen is this? He cautiously approached his desk where the Raven appeared to be reading, but as soon as he stood beside the creature, the Raven lifted its head, its eyes, a blaring green, staring into his very soul.

"A-are you real? Why are you here?" The eyes never moved from his. "Must you stare at me like that?"

The Raven cocked its head, considering the question, and to the man's surprise, the beak opened not to utter the familiar melodical croak, but to reveal the voice of a female to reply, "Nevermore."

"You spoke!" The man exclaimed. "You spoke and answered my question, but what does it mean? What do you mean by 'nevermore'?"

The Raven hopped across the desk, its nails clicking along, to a necklace, lying by the portrait, that once belonged to the dearly departed Lenore, and curled its claw around the item. "Nevermore," she repeated.

After a few moments of silent regard, the man laughed heartily at his own train of thought, believing the bird was here to impart some message of importance, as it stared at him with terrifically human eyes. "You merely have a penchant for shiny trinkets. You aren't here for some great importance. Merely a bird seeking warmth from the winter air, and nothing more."

The bird looped the necklace around its own neck and hopped delicately atop the portrait. The man swore the Raven narrowed her eyes in a sense of knowing. "Nevermore."

An unnatural bout of rage coursed through the man. "What are you? Why are you here? Has God sent you? Or perhaps the Devil? Here to torture me over the death of my beloved?!"

"Nevermore."

The man picked up the nearest object and hurled it at the fowl, who merely tipped its head to miss the impact. "Leave. Leave now! Cease reminding me of her! Unless you've come to tell me about her death, then stop reminding me of that night! I' have done well to forget all that has happened but now the memories are flooding back. I implore you, foul beast of Beelzebub, leave me at once!"

"Nevermore," the bird responded, in a more mockingly, melodic tone.

He was dumbfounded, staring intensely at this bird who had yet to flinch, still staring into his soul, judging him in silence as if she knew all of his secrets. All he had to do was reach out and grab the beast by the neck to end it all, but he couldn't bring himself to get any closer, instead, he placed as much space as he could between them. His anger was reaching a boiling point, his blood pressure rising quicker than the tides, and a great pain began to fill his heaving chest. "Raven. Fowl of the night. I don't know how you know, but I ask you. Why did you come?"

"Nevermore."

He gripped at his left breast, the pain getting worse. "Say something else. Anything else."

"Nevermore."

His vision began to blur, and white streaks framed his sight. "Say something else! Say something of importance!"

"Nevermore."

"Stop mocking me with this!" He spluttered, saliva dribbling down his chin. "Tell me! You must tell me! WHY ARE YOU HE--" In a great wave of pain, the man dropped to his knees, his eyes clenched tight.

The Raven cocked her head in a smug interest as the man collapsed onto the floor, lying, writhing on his back.

"Nevermore," the Raven repeated.

In the man's heated gaze, he observed the corvid grow in size until it resembled a human female, hair and dress as dark as the feathers once covering her, and eyes... the same piercing green. The woman looked down at him, then looked to the door.

"You may come in, ma'am. The deed you requested is done."

A shrouded female entered the man's field of vision. "You did it," she breathed in disbelief. She removed her hood to reveal a cascade of fair brown hair, and orbs of blue, cheeks flushed rose, and lips full.

"L-L-Len--" the man spluttered, mustering all the strength he could to say her name, before his spirit left the Earthly plain, "Len...ore..."

"You really did it. He's dead! He's dead, isn't he?!" Lenore asked with glee.

"Of course, ma'am. I always complete a job. May I ask, was my performance satisfactory?"

"Oh yes!" Lenore exclaimed. "Ever since he left me for dead in those woods, I wanted nothing more but revenge. No one searched for me. It was as if he made everyone forget I ever existed. Those years I spend surviving on my lonesome, becoming a barbaric woods-woman. Oh, my elation when I rediscovered society, and people! Oh, how I missed people! But no one knew who I was. No one dared believe who I was." She buried her head in her hands. "I can't believe I loved him once, with all my heart. The naivety of youth."

The Raven, a mystical shapeshifter with a cause and knack for creative assassination, placed a slender, porcelain white hand on Lenore's shoulder, comforting the long-suffering woman. "And now, the world shall forget about him as well. From this point on, he never existed, ma'am. Another tall tale to scare children at night, much like how you were."

"I cannot thank you enough." Lenore sobbed. Her gaze then lingered upon the pendant around Raven's neck.

"Apologies ma'am, I never took it off." Raven undid the clasp with her long nails, and delicately held it out. "I'm sure you would like it back, no?"

Lenore stared at the pendant with fondness, that quickly turned to absolute disgust. "Leave it. Leave it to gather dust. I want no reminder of him. It was a marriage gift... more of a curse in the end. I never want to lay eyes on it again."

Raven smiled, and wrapped her fingers around the pendant. "Then, I believe, I have found my payment. Quite a piece." Her eyes glistened. "The energy surrounding it, oh yes. Would you mind, if I accepted this as payment?"

Lenore smiled softly. "Not at all, Raven. You deserve the world for what you've done for me."

"Then I suggest we go, ma'am. I shall leave the body here per your request. Let his demise be the mystery yours once was."

Raven didn't bother to step over the man, but used him more as a welcome mat, to make her way out the door. She never knew the man personally, but when told of how he attempted to kill Lenore, leaving her for dead, and through his charm and intellect convinced the town he knew nothing of her disappearance... and was quick to take on the role of a grieving widow, she knew in her heart the despicable man he was. He believed his role to dearly he became what he pretended to be. The man truly believed he knew not what happened to his dear Lenore, and pined for her night after night. Raven knew just how to break the man, as deep down she knew his remembrance of what he had done was still there, and could easily be brought to the surface. Looking down at his now lifeless body, Raven wiped her shoes off on his shirt, and found a smile spreading across her face. Not all jobs felt as satisfactory as this one.

The weather outside seemed to take a break from its chilly atmosphere, and a feeling of warmth overtook Lenore. Happiness. This was what happiness felt like. Her smile couldn't get any wider, it seemed, as such a feeling hadn't consumed her in many, many years.

The darkness outside lifted to expose a shower of stars, a dazzling display the shore hasn't seen in decades. The waves ceased their angry crashing and settled into calming laps upon the sand. The glow of candles from inside the house became an eerie beacon in the dead of night, one that no one would see or pay a passing glance, as no one visited the shore, not to see the man... and not since Lenore.

The women left the small abode by the shore, where the man would live, nevermore.

JESSICA CHALEFF

Jessica Chalefff is an avid lover of all things horror and sci-fi. These genres tend to blossom through writing, as well as art. She currently lives at home, hunched over a laptop, constantly writing. Jessica can be found interacting with people through social media almost daily! You can find her on Twitter, Facebook, Instagram, YouTube, and even Etsy. Just look up TimeLassCreations, or TheTimeLass, and look for a bow-tied clock a bowler hat!

"A Christmas Reckoning"

A Christmas Carol

Mike L Lane

Jacob Marley was dead as a doornail.

Still.

There was no doubt whatsoever about it. He still wandered the grounds near his old lending house—his hair, skirts and tassels whipping in the palpable brown air and covered in black soot, his face emitting a phosphorescent glow like rotting crayfish in a darkened cellar. The heavy chains he unknowingly forged in life dragged behind him like a linked tail, wound and clasped tight around his waist, bearing the burdens of countless ledgers, cash-boxes, safes, deeds, purses, padlocks and keys. His jaw was still bound in the folded handkerchief wrapped about his head and chin—not to keep his mouth from gaping as before, but to stop it from falling off of his face entirely as rot and decay had eroded its marrow hinges. Fraught with misery, he still wailed his frightful, anguished cries corralled amongst other mourning specters suffering similar fates. The multitude grew daily as the surplus population spilled into the afterlife. A vast majority of these souls held Marley accountable for their torments, screeching indignations at him, tugging on his chains and clawing at his throat. Doomed to wander through the world, eternity stretched out before him like the Thames flowing into the North Sea and beyond with no end in sight.

Yes. Old Marley was still dead as a doornail, but it wasn't supposed to be this way—not after the second chance he procured for Ebenezer.

Silver-tongued and bowelless, Marley was a shrewd businessman, even in the afterlife. If Ebenezer's name was good upon 'Change, Marley's was not. His slippery tongue secured many a contract and weaseled out

138

of just as many as long as he and his partner were compensated handsomely. Where Scrooge manipulated numbers to work in their favor, Marley manipulated the people. It was his gift. He was the king of persuasion, loosely wording his contracts like a bad young Act of Parliament should he ever need an escape clause. The hereafter was no different.

It had taken him seven years to find a possible loophole in his afterlife arrangement—sitting invisible beside Ebenezer daily while pleading with the three Spirits on his partner's behalf—before the opportunity was granted. Worst case scenario, he assumed Scrooge would die of fright and keep him company throughout eternity. Misery did indeed love company, and it was only right. Ebenezer deserved to share blame among these hostile souls they had both nudged toward the wrong side of life's ledger. But if all went as planned, Marley's efforts to change the old miser's heart wouldn't go unrewarded. Perhaps his deed would earn him a pardon, releasing him from this everlasting torment.

His plan had worked far better than he expected, too. After Scrooge's confrontation with the Spirits—Jacob Marley being the first and foremost—Ebenezer had indeed seen the error of his ways. He became a new man altogether, shedding the chains of his former life through good deeds and kindness for the next seven years. He had managed to avoid Marley's fate, shuffling off his mortal coil one night surrounded by family and friends.

With a seething glare from his death-cold eyes, Marley moved through the crowd of tortured souls and stared at the counting house, the reality bearing down on him like a locomotive hearse. The sign above the warehouse door no longer read Scrooge & Marley, but Cratchit & Sons. Bob Cratchit—the same groveling clerk Marley hired long ago for next to nothing—had inherited the business and fortune Marley had worked so hard to procure, along with two of his children, Peter and Timothy. It seemed everyone benefited from Ebenezer's reformation.

Everyone but Old Marley.

"Your idea was a complete success, Jacob," the Ghost of Christmas Past said, adjusting the extinguisher's cap on his head. Marley often visited Past, since memories were all he had left to hold onto. Reliving glimpses from his life provided a slight reprieve from this miserable existence, so he often begged Past for a peek beneath the cap and to his credit, Past allowed it from time to time. He could get lost in the bright jet of light emitting from the crown of Past's head. "You gave Ebenezer a second chance on life! Because of your help, he was no longer a man of business, but made mankind his business through charity, mercy, forbearance, and benevolence! His old ways would have surely condemned him to your side for eternity, dragging about chains heavier than your own, I'm afraid. You should be proud of the accomplishment! The world over knows the story of Ebenezer and the three Christmas Spirits!"

"Humbug!" Jacob spat, clanking his chains in fury. Past recoiled from Marley's outcry, dropping the sprig of holly and gathering the flowered hem of his white tunic in hand. Terrified, a whirlwind of anguished souls fled from the area in a spectral scatter. "The world knows, eh? Knows how you showed Ebenezer his youth to remind him of what he no longer was? How the Ghost of Christmas Present showed him a sick child he could save if only he changed his ways? How the Ghost of Christmas Yet to Come instilled fear within an old man over a death he couldn't possibly avoid no matter what path he took in life?"

"I suppose that's one way of looking at it," Past admitted, retrieving the holly sprig from the frozen ground. As he bent, light streamed from beneath his cap, flooding Marley's mind with memories long forgotten and better days he would never experience again. The brilliance of the Spirit's light held Marley in a captive trance until Past stood upright and readjusted his hat.

Marley regained his composure and pressed on.

"And what do they say of me, Spirit? I have wandered the earth. I have heard Ebenezer's story on the lips of the living for some time now. Do you know what they all say? Ask any living soul how many visitors Scrooge received on that fateful night and the answer is always three! Even you yourself just claimed—with much pride, I might add—that Ebenezer was changed by the three Christmas Spirits, when in fact there were four! It was I who made the plea for my partner! I was the buffer for you and the other Spirits! It was I who showed him his inevitable afterlife! If not for me, the old fool would have continued on his miserable path undeterred. He would be standing with us now, mourning as I mourn. Wailing as I wail. Suffering as I suffer!"

"What you say is true, Jacob," Past replied with an amiable shrug. "The past can never lie."

The childlike grin beaming beneath the Spirit's long white hair made Marley's jaw clench. He cinched the handkerchief tighter around his head to keep the crumbling bones from falling out. It seemed he must keep his head about him in more ways than one.

"If Ebenezer was rewarded for his good deeds, should I not be recompensed as well?"

"It seems only right," Past agreed. "You should've mentioned this in your proposal, Jacob. I'm sure something could have been arranged."

"Surely, it is a debt owed to me," he replied, moving in close and placing an arm around the Spirit's shoulders. A twinkle of the old lender's persuasive powers sparkled in Marley's dead, cold eyes. "For services rendered, of course. Couldn't certain arrangements be made now?"

"The past cannot be changed," Past shrugged, cutting his eyes toward the glow beneath his cap. "You, of all souls, know the rules."

He had anticipated as much from the Spirit—the past was the past, after all, and yesteryear made for a stubborn bedfellow, iron-willed and set in its ways—but this wasn't Marley's first negotiation. He set his pitch.

"Perhaps we could convene with the others?" he proposed, his arm still around Past's shoulders. "You know everyone so well, Past, perhaps you could speak on my behalf?"

"It is very rare we all meet at once," Past frowned. As he thought it over, white bushy brows furrowed on the unblemished face. "Even with Scrooge's intervention we were never together at the same time. In fact, I only see the Ghost of Christmas Yet to Come when he believes I need immediate forewarning. As for Present, I always just miss him. He dies every day, you know, only to be replaced by a newborn brother. I can't say I envy his job, living such a short life and forced to restrain those two heathen children, Ignorance and Want."

Wheels began to turn in Marley's head. It was a rash thought, little more than a flashing image in his mind—nothing he would act on, of course—but it was there nonetheless. He could summon Yet to Come by simply wrapping his chains around Past's delicate throat. Even the mere thought of placing the Spirit in danger might be enough.

"If we were to gather them, do you believe they would grant me a reprieve?" he asked, pulling him in closer with a friendly squeeze. His other hand groped for the chain at his back. "Would they acknowledge my good deed and release me from these bonds?"

"I cannot lie," Past replied, the simple smile fading from his lips. "I can only judge you by your past indiscretions, and you were far worse than Scrooge ever was. Present is so fickle, it's doubtful he would give you a pass without me. And Yet to Come never speaks, but with the point of his finger he can only show you what could be, not what will be."

"Then there is no hope for me?" Marley asked, masking his rage with one last plea. His clutch on the chain grew tighter, the image of it wrapped around the Spirit's throat repeating over and over again in his mind.

"Your best chance lies with Present. He must be nearby," Past said. He surveyed the grounds around the lending house in search of the Spirit when his eyes landed on another. "What are you doing here?"

The Ghost of Christmas Yet to Come materialized in the bleak fog. Cloaked and hooded, the Spirit silently approached them like a rolling mist blanketing the grounds, gloom and misery following in his wake. The phantom was as dark as the inkblot signatures staining the ledgers hooked to Marley's chains. Jacob shivered in the solemn dread the Spirit's presence evoked, the chain links clattering behind him like a housemaid dropping a tray of silverware. His plan was working. He cultivated the murderous thought in his mind—picturing the tender bloom on Past's cheeks turning shades of purple, the chains cutting into his flesh, his tongue lolling from his mouth, his eyes glazing over like ice—until he was certain Yet to Come must show his fellow Spirit the warning.

Yet to Come pointed a long, gnarled finger at Past, the Spirit's probable future unfolding before him. His eyes grew as bright as the light beneath his cap, stunned and drawn to the images Yet to Come projected, unable to look away. Before the Spirit could withdraw his finger, Marley made his move.

Quicker than a man could say Jack Robinson, Marley snatched the extinguisher's cap from Past's head, releasing a beacon of light into the shrouded face of Yet to Come. The phantom Spirit's pitch black sockets basked in the rays beaming from Past's exposed head as nearby souls flocked to see memory's light—a glorious reprieve from their lamentations.

Jacob Marley kept his eyes on the hard, frozen earth, a wicked smirk spreading on his face.

Past was trapped gawking into the future like a spellbound lover, and Yet to Come mimicked Past's daze, staring into the shadow of things that had been, but he had never seen. Like drugged mental patients at Bedlam, the two Spirits locked gazes, trapped in the mental straight coats Marley had conjured—the loophole the old lender anticipated.

"Enjoy one another's company," Marley fumed, careful not to stare into the light lest he find himself mesmerized by his own past. He placed the cap within one of the safes attached to his chains, locking it away for safekeeping. "I pray for both your sakes, the Ghost of Christmas Present has a more satisfactory answer for me. I am owed a debt I will collect."

He fled from the horde of souls surrounding Past and Yet to Come, slipping through the crowd and making his way around to the back of the counting house, pressing business on his mind. In his haste, he ran right into a tall, young Spirit—an adolescent boy caught between the death throes of childhood and the verge of becoming a man—wearing a green robe twice his size and a holly wreath upon his head. Jacob toppled to the ground, fuming. With a beaming smile, the Spirit offered Marley a hand up.

"I do believe you have never seen the like of me before!" the Spirit exclaimed, his eyes sparkling. He placed a large hand on Jacob's shoulder to steady the old soul.

"I have urgent business to attend to," Marley scowled. "Unhand me!"

"Off in a rush, I see," the Spirit said with a cheery voice. He removed his grip from Jacob's shoulder and brushed dust from the white fur trimming his robe. "I admire a soul with such urgency! Such initiative! As my brothers before me have always said, there's no time like the present!"

Marley realized at once that Past was right. The Ghost of Christmas Present was indeed always near.

"Forgive me, Spirit! It is you I am so eager to see," Marley said, casting a furtive glance behind him. The wails of the damned surrounding Past and Yet to Come grew louder around the corner, and he knew he must act fast before Present discovered what he had done. "I know your time is limited—your short life having only just begun—but I once worked with one of your brothers nearly seven years ago, and it pains me to say, I have a grievance only you can rectify."

"By all means," the Ghost said in a booming, but friendly voice. His hair grew longer as he spoke, the dark brown curls hanging loose and free about his shoulders. Stubble emerged from his chin. "How can I help you?"

"I feel like I was choused as ever a poor devil has been," Jacob explained. The Spirit leaned his head toward the ruckus, his interest piqued, but Marley maneuvered himself forward to block his view. "I helped the three Spirits—Past, Present and Yet to Come—reform an old partner of mine. Though you were just born this very day, I assume you know the story of Ebenezer Scrooge?"

"A fine tale! Who hasn't heard of the old miser's miraculous change of heart? Everyone knows of the three Christmas Spirits and their charitable deed! And you say you helped them in some way?"

"Yes," Marley replied through clenched teeth. "I am Jacob Marley. If you've heard the tale, you must know of me."

"Ah, yes! The doorknocker! Splendid trick you pulled there, though I must admit I'm not sure how that helped the poor fellow. It must have given him quite the fright."

For the first time in a very long while, Marley's cold soul felt the flames of rage roaring deep within him.

"I am more than just a door fixture in the story! I was the one who acted on Scrooge's behalf," he pressed on, trying his best to maintain composure beneath the Spirit's insult. "I made the arrangements, introduced him to the Spirits and set him on his newfound path. Yet I received nothing for my efforts. I am owed."

"Perhaps you are," Present mused, scratching the beard growing before Marley's eyes. "Though I don't see what it has to do with me. You should have bargained with the Spirits back then. I only deal in the here and now, as you know."

Marley stewed in his fury. He was afraid it would come to this. None of the Spirits would give him his due satisfaction—no freedom from this bondage, not even an offer to shed some of the weight from his chains. It was an outrage.

"Never live in the past," the Spirit said, reading the angry expression on Marley's face. The condescending pat on Jacob's back only served to stoke the flames. "You should always live for the moment."

"I thought you might say that," Jacob seethed, shaking his head. "I have another question. Are you still responsible for those two wretched children, Ignorance and Want?"

"I am," the Ghost replied solemnly. His robe opened and two hideous children lunged forward, trying to escape. The boy, known as Ignorance, growled at Jacob and the girl, Want, stretched out her hands toward him. The Ghost of Christmas Present placed a firm hand on each child's shoulder to restrain them.

"They appear to be a handful," Jacob said, eyeing them with utter disgust. They were truly wretched, ravenous creatures—meagre, ragged and wolfish in their demeanor. Though they were mere children, their faces were marred, pinched and twisted by the stale touch of old age. "Tell me, Spirit, why do you restrain them? Are they yours?"

"No, they are the children of Man. They are the bringers of doom to all mankind, especially the boy. It is my sworn duty to hold them back lest they run amuck within the world."

"So I've heard," Jacob said, patting Ignorance on his mangy head. The feral boy snapped sharp teeth at him, and Marley recoiled in horror. The sickly girl craned her neck forward with a neglected pout, but Marley dared not touch her. "This may be a little rude, but how much time do you have left, Spirit? Before your life ends and your new brother's life begins?"

"I have half the day still," the Ghost beamed. His optimistic view made Marley loathe him all the more. He was glad. It dissolved any resignations he had about what he must do.

"And I suppose he would not help me either?"

If Marley couldn't collect what was owed him, he would find another way to make them pay. It was the unwritten rule of lending.

"I'm sure he would not," the Spirit admitted with a dismissive shrug, his broad smile never faltering. "But do not look so glum, old fellow! Don't dwell on the past, but take action! Seize the day!"

The wailing shrieks of the nearby souls grew louder, and he brushed past Marley, curious to see why so many souls were gathering behind the counting house.

"What is causing such a ruckus back there?"

With no time left to lose and no reward to be gained, Jacob made his move.

He swung the heavy chain around Present's neck and strangled him with all of his might. The man child put forth a valiant effort—so much so, Marley wondered if his strength would be enough to win out—but in the end, it was the overbearing weight of his chains that crushed the Spirit's throat. Amid the struggle, the little monstrosities scampered from Present's robe, fleeing into the world like stark raving lunatics, eager to sow their evil seeds. Before completely leaving his sight, Ignorance looked back at Jacob Marley, his eyes aglow as he snarled. A wicked grin spread across his twisted face.

"Run, little one!" Jacob said, easing Present's dead body to the ground. The Spirit's tongue lolled from his mouth, and his eyes bulged from their sockets in a permanent state of shock. "Spread your sickness throughout the world! Curse them, each and every one! If I must suffer for an eternity, I'll dare not do it alone."

MIKE L. LANE

M ike L Lane straddles two planes of existence—the boring, mundane world we all mill around in from day to day and the vast universes of the written word where escape from the daily grind is merely a page turn or pen stroke away. He prefers the latter, gorging on all things horror, especially in his writing. Inspired at an early age by the likes of Stephen King (cliché I know, but true nonetheless), Charles Dickens, Edgar Alan Poe, Flannery O'Connor, Ray Bradbury and Robert R McCammon, Mike believes the best stories can only be told by realistic characters and all of their flaws. Operating strictly under the code of character driven storytelling, Mike claws through the sludge of his macabre riddled brain in hopes of finding the truths in life only good horror can expose. Sometimes, when he's feeling extra dark, he even likes to draw the creatures conjured from his imagination. He is currently working on a collection of stories he plans to unleash on this unsuspecting world very soon, but in the meantime he stays hidden within the realms of darkness, a spider spinning his webs, biding his time and hoping you'll stop by and say hello.

Web- http://mikellane.com/

Facebook- https://www.facebook.com/MikeLLaneAuthor

Amazon- https://www.amazon.com/author/mikelane

ALICE FALLS INTO WONDERLAND
ALICE IN WONDERLAND

Ross Ellison

Children wandering around lost in thought is a normal situation. But one little girl found herself in quite an abnormal situation. Certainly not a normal day. This child found her pacing stopped by a burly man. She had never met him.

"You're Alice right?" The burly man smelled of danger. Best to turn around and never speak to him again.

Yet as she turned about, Alice had no idea where "here" was. Her troubles only increased with a second voice. A second stranger.

"Alice. We know you are scared. But try to stay calm."

"I don't talk to strangers." she scoffed. "It's improper and only leads to trouble. Didn't your parents tell you that?" She left without another word for these two. Even if she was walking the wrong way, better to be away from these men who knew her name.

"Alice dear. We can take you to your family. Just turn back around and let us explain."

She was done with their games. Let them chase her if they cared so much about her well being. She took off in a sprint, no longer concerned that she wore the absolute worst dress for running.

Oh dear. My dress will be a mess when I get home.

Images of home flashed before her eyes. She so desperately wanted to be out of this situation. How had she found her way here at all? Why was she being chased by strange men? If she made it back to safety that wouldn't matter.

Unfortunately, her feet lost their footing. A hole managed to wedge itself between safety and she fell. If this was the lair of a snake, it was no reptile she wanted to meet!

Alice spun through the dirt, certain that her dress was completely ruined. Her blond hair grabbed all the dirt as she tumbled into a deep hole. The light above quickly vanished and soon enough, the poor girl was in the dark.

That was until something stopped her from rolling. But what had Alice found? It didn't feel like a rock. As she touched whatever had prevented her from going farther, there was no dirt to touch. Instead, a smooth barrier blocked her way.

"Oh no. Am I trapped in this hole? With no way out? Help!" She shouted, no longer worried about her pursuers.

The girl feared that she was alone in the dark, but a sudden voice calmed her nerves. Whoever this stranger was, they held a light too. They moved quite fast. The light seemed so far away at first, but as if like magic, suddenly moved past her and revealed her surroundings.

Alice found herself in a dark cave. And the barrier that had stopped her fall? A door. But after that, things stopped making sense. She prided herself on intelligence. Alice had followed her classes and reading to a T. So when she spotted a small rabbit holding a lantern and a pocket watch, she didn't know how to react.

"I'm late! I'm late!" The rabbit cried and only as she got over the shock of understanding his speech, did she also realize he stood on his hind legs. Like a person would.

"Excuse me umm mister…"

"I can't talk. Not now! I'm late. The Queen will have my head for sure!" Alice noticed that the rabbit grabbed a doorknob far too low for her to even notice. A small entrance appeared below and the rabbit sped inside leaving her once again in the dark.

Now, what did she do? Once again alone, Alice thought through what to do. She could try climbing back up, but that might not be possible. Not to mention that those strange men still were nearby. She didn't want to run into them. Especially covered in dirt like she was now.

"Oh, mother! Father! Where are you? Poor Alice is all alone and scared!"

She hadn't expected to get any sort of response, but to her surprise, she managed to attract the attention of someone. Though she couldn't figure out who, or where they were.

"Would you please stop shouting?" A droll voice requested. "I'm trying to sleep." The speaker even fought yawns back while complaining.

"It's rude to yawn while speaking." Alice declared. "Not to mention talking to someone in the dark. Who are you? Where are you?"

"I'm right in front of you. Now please I'm still trying to sleep."

"In front of me? But all I saw was a door"

"Yes. And I'm the doorknob."

"A talking doorknob? There shouldn't be such a thing."

"I beg your pardon. You mean to say you have never spoken to a door-knob before?"

"I have never done anything so strange in my life." She was talking to a doorknob. It even gave off some light. "But how do I get out of here? I'm trapped you see."

"Well." He yawned far too obnoxiously for Alice's liking. "I suggest you use the door the way it was intended. Open it up and go through."

"But the door is much too small!" Alice protested. She wasn't wrong. The rabbit, while loud and shouting enough to fill up a much larger space, was much smaller than she.

"No." The door interjected. "You are simply too big."

But what was she to do then? The tunnel back only led to those mysterious men. Alice only became more convinced by the minute that they meant her harm. Did she risk returning to them? She might starve in this cave if she couldn't get through that door.

"Oh dear oh dear!" She fought back tears and ran from the glowing door and back into the darkness. "Help me! Someone!" Her cries only reverberated off the walls.

"Please keep it down. I need to sleep." The doorknob mentioned again. Yet how could she still hear him if she had run far away from that wall? Stranger still, his voice seemed louder and above her rather than below.

Alice turned around and saw the door. Now she could fit through. But how could that be? Had she shrunk? Had the door grown to accommodate her?

"Hurry up." The doorknob yawned between words. "I'm truly exhausted now."

"Oh, thank you, sir." Alice had to jump to grab the handle properly and the larger size felt awkward as her hands wrapped around the golden bronze.

"Finally..." was the only statement of a farewell the girl received as the door behind shut. But where was she now?

She needed to blink to avoid going blind. She had been in the dark for quite a long time. When her eyes finally adjusted, she saw a checkerboard road that dove this way and that between curved walls.

"I'm laaate! The Queen will have my head!" The rabbit had not made much headway given how quickly his shouts reached her.

"Excuse me!" She called out. "Who is this queen?"

"The Queen of Hearts!" He continued to run and Alice desperate for some idea of her location followed. "Her majesty is the most beautiful and just soul!"

Unfortunately, Alice was not dressed for running and the Rabbit's shouts grew fainter as she stumbled into a large room. Looking at the table that cast a large shadow, she convinced herself that somehow the girl had shrunk. But how could that be? People didn't just shrink? That was well... something that happened in books.

"Have I entered a book?" She asked, though of course, no one was there to answer. Well, not quite as it turned out.

"If a girl shouts in an empty room and no one hears it, did she make a peep?" Alice turned around and came face to face with not a face at all. Just a wide-toothed grin.

"Well, you heard me didn't you?" She was far too confused to even properly ask who this grinning face belonged to.

"Did I hear? I'm not sure if I did."

"That doesn't make any sense. If you didn't hear me, how did you know to respond?"

"Did I know to respond? Maybe I'm just saying gibberish and it happens to make sense to you." The face vanished and Alice was left feeling taken aback.

"Who are you?" She was desperate for some semblance of logic. Nothing in the time since she fell down this hole made any.

"Why don't you ask where you are?" A full-face materialized this time. The face of a cat. At least, Alice thought it was a cat.

"A cat? But I have never seen a cat without a body before."

"Am I a cat? Are you sure that's a word and not just a sound your mouth made that sounds soothing?" The cat purred as if knowing its statement made no sense.

"Ok... umm... where am I?"

"That depends." The "maybe cat" answered. "Where do you want to be?" The face vanished again.

"But where I want to be is out there!" Alice wanted to go home. She needed to be back home safe above all else. This bizarre place filled with talking animals and vanishing cats felt dangerous and, well, it just felt weird.

She turned away from the spot that the cat vanished into and went back towards the door. Unfortunately, she met another conundrum.

"Oh no! I never stopped shrinking!" The door was far too high up now. She couldn't reach it, no matter how high she jumped. And there was nowhere to climb on this side of the door.

Deciding that there was nothing good coming from this direction, she returned to where she met the cat. Yet, somehow she missed that place when she ventured down the twisted hall for a second time. She stood in a forest now. But how could that be? One simply didn't miss places.

A strange scent flew at her nose tickling her insides. Alice sneezed hoping that whatever allergen had struck so was gone now. Only for the smoke to form again. Where was it coming from?

As she tried to find the source, her lungs filled with the stuff as well. Coughing and gagging now, Alice desperately strove forward to figure out what the cause of this smoke was.

At the end of the path, with trees creating a hallway all around, she found another creature. And it was smoking. Smoking. Her mother had always taught her smoking was a bad behavior that only those who had a deathwish partook in.

"Excuse me. Could you please..." she suppressed more coughing as the smoke rushed into her lungs. "Could you please stop smoking that?"

Whoever this individual was, they didn't listen. Alice realized while trying to figure out who this person was, and more importantly why they were ignoring her, that this smoker had a few features different from everything else here.

Notably, he was a Caterpillar. At least the cat and rabbit had been mammals like her. She assumed it was a he since women were far too smart to smoke.

"Where am I?" She dared ask. Still unhappy that the Caterpillar ignored her and continued sending smoke that kept choking her lungs her way.

"Who... are... you?" He finally stated, but if it was directed her way, he didn't make it obvious.

"I would very much like to know where I am." She tried to correct his question back towards one she desperately needed to know.

"No. Who... are you?" So he was listening.

"I don't talk to strangers." She claimed, but now she was lying. The Doorknob, Rabbit, and Cat had all been strangers too.

"We aren't strangers." He managed to make every syllable sound rude. "Why else would we be speaking otherwise?"

"Well. Umm," This place continued to fluster the poor girl. "I'm Alice." She tried her best to courtsy and earned more smoke in her lungs as a parting gift.

"Who are you?" He asked again. That was, despite her already answering.

"I already told you. I'm Alice."

"That is a name." The Caterpillar droned on. "I asked, who are you?"

"I don't know?" She answered wondering if the Caterpillar was just crazy.

"Well then go see the Queen. She knows who everyone is." Even while exchanging in conversation, he blew more smoke in her face.

"Where can I find this Queen?"

'Not any Queen, the Red Queen. She is the most beautiful and caring ruler in all the land."

"Where can I find her?"

"In her court. Thataway." He pointed with his tail. His tail. That was like if she pointed with her feet. Also, he pointed back towards where she came from.

"Thank you?" She asked and answered at the same time. He chose to ignore her again. Alice paced back through the strange forest, back towards the door that was too big once again.

Except once again, she managed to miss where she had been. This time, she found a gate made of hedges. Hedges guarded by people that looked like cards. Card Soldiers?

"Halt." One of them commanded. "What business have you in the Queen's Court?"

"I came to see the Queen." Alice lied. Didn't her parents warn her against that? Lies had this habit of coming back to bite you. That is what her mother had always claimed.

"Should we let her through?" One of the card soldiers whispered to the other. Yet he spoke loud enough for the girl to hear.

"I came to tell her something important." Remembering the words spoken by the Rabbit, the poor girl lied a second time in desperation to get through this obstacle.

"Well if it's important, you may pass," answered one.

"Remember to respect the Red Queen. She is the most beautiful in all the land," added the other.

Alice wondered just what sort of person this Red Queen was. That was now twice that someone in this bizarre place had described her with such praise.

Well, it didn't take long for her to see the Queen. She had no problem announcing her presence for all the area to hear.

"Order in the court!" Her voice did not sound beautiful at all. Rather the speaker sounded strained as if yelling for hours.

"But my Queen, she is nowhere to be found." Alice knew that voice. It was the Rabbit

The Red Queen sat upon a throne and held a gavel in her right hand. This was a court. A court of law. Alice didn't know much about these sort of places, but her father loved speaking about them.

"Nowhere to be found?" The Queen stood up and glared down at the poor rabbit. "Do you know what happens to those who defy me?"

"Yes, my Queen. I didn't realize her importance when I ran past." He seemed to shrink with every word.

"Yet you ignored the intruder. An intruder who poses a threat to ME. YOUR QUEEN!" It was terrifying how quickly the Red Queen went from quiet to furious.

"Umm, excuse me." Alice dared to add herself to the situation.

"Who are you?" The Queen noticed the girl immediately.

"My name is Alice and I-"

"Stop right there. I know of no Alice. Nor do I have an appointment with one. Please leave."

"But-"

"Do you dare defy me!? I AM THE RED QUEEN!!" Alice shrunk back just like the rabbit. There was little beauty to be found in the Queen. She struck as more of an angry and violent sort.

"My Queen." The Rabbit attempted to interject. "That girl is-"

"Did I tell you to speak? Defy me again and it will be off with your head!"

"But she is the intruder!"

The Queen's face made a frightening turn. First, she focused her fury at the rabbit, then the anger vanished from her face. This in turn was replaced by a smile. A cruel smile that foreshadowed pain. Then that same smile mutated into a frown as she turned towards Alice.

"Girl. Why have you invaded my Kingdom? This fair land knows only peace. Yet you have caused chaos with every step."

"I have done no such thing." Though she had lied to get in here, Alice spoke only the truth now.

"Oh really? Rabbit. Bring out the list of crimes."

"Yes, my Queen." No longer did the Rabbit shrink in her presence. Instead, it was her turn to shrink as he pulled a scroll from who knows where. As the parchment unfurled it ran across the court and shifted to and fro. Finally, it ended at Alice's feet.

"That can't be!" Alice cried. I only just got here."

"She lies, my Queen. The parchment is proof of that. Would you like me to read it?"

"No need." The Queen answered. "We already know of her crimes."

"But that's not fair!" Alice surmised. "Don't I get to hear what crimes I committed?"

"Should I add that crime to the list, my Queen?"

The Red Queen did not listen to the rabbit. Instead, she scowled towards Alice. "You. Dare. Defy. Me? I AM THE RED QUEEN! I will have order in my court and lands! There is no need for a trial! Off with her head!"

Alice didn't know what she had hoped would happen by meeting the queen, but being killed for a crime she hadn't committed had not been what she expected. Not wanting to die, she looked for a quick exit. Maybe if she ran fast, she could escape the queen.

"After her!" The Red Queen screeched as Alice ran through another door. The path back to the forest was still guarded so that left her only this option. She wasn't sure what she would discover in this bizarre land. Things had stopped making sense as soon as she fell down that hole.

Wait. Things hadn't made sense before that either. How had she ended up so far away from home? Why had those two men chased her into the hole in the first place? How had they known her name?

The worst part had to be the queen though. Alice had run away to this strange place to avoid danger and instead had charged right in. She didn't know what those men in the world above would do to her, but the Red Queen sounded serious about beheading.

"Well, are you just gonna stand there? Take a seat!" A new voice dragged her away from racing thoughts. In her haste, Alice had not stopped to look at her surroundings.

"I think she's mad in the head." The first speaker had at least appeared human, though with a large hat that made him look silly. The second though was another rabbit. Though this one looked nothing like the servant of the Queen.

"Where am I?" She dared ask, wondering if she would like the answer this time.

"You are at our tea party. Please take a seat. I'm the Mad Hatter." He attempted to bow but stopped short before his hat collided with the table.

"I'm the March Hare." The Rabbit added.

The girl decided to take a seat. She needed some tea after all the running and excitement. Fear of death notwithstanding of course.

"A toast!" The Mad Hatter shouted so loud that Alice feared that he would summon the Queen's guards.

"To what?" She asked.

"To our unbirthdays of course" The March Hare chimed.

"Unbirthday?"

"Well, every day that isn't your birthday is your unbirthday. We get to celebrate almost every day!" The Mad Hatter continued to shout, though Alice wished he would stay quiet.

"That's nice I suppose."

"Oh is it your birthday today?" The March Hare seemed more sensible than his companion.

"I- I don't know." How could she have forgotten something so important? The more she tried to remember, the more she realized she had forgotten. "I don't understand."

"Understand what Alice?" The Mad Hatter asked.

"Wait! How do you know my name?"

"Oh, the Queen told us you were coming. This is her jail after all." The March Hare's words forced a lump in her throat.

"The Queens... Jail?"

"Oh yes." The Mad Hatter was no longer shouting. "I have been trapped in this place for so long that I am quite strikingly mad." He laughed at the words, but Alice could sense despair in his words.

"We celebrate our unbirthdays because the Queen trapped us here with our punishment being that we will never reach April."

"She can do that?" Alice didn't know how anyone could do such a thing.

"Of course I can. I am the Red Queen. The Ruler and most beautiful person in the realm!" The Red Queen appeared in the clearing. She was flanked by a stack of card soldiers.

Alice didn't think there was a single lovely thing about her. She wondered if she was doomed no matter what and felt brave enough to defy this woman.

"There isn't a single lovely thing about you. You are..." The words she needed eluded her. "You're a big meany!"

"Guards! I will not allow this child to tarnish our realm any longer! Off with her head! NOW!"

Alice heard a chorus of wind and card soldiers appeared all around her. They were surprisingly strong for beings made of, well, whatever they were made of. She tried to break free of their grip, but nothing could be done.

One of the soldiers lifted his ax and she knew this was the end. Alice made eye contact with the Red Queen one final time and glared hatred the best she could. Goodbye Mom. Goodbye Dad.

"Sounds like the process is complete." Tweedle Dee told his companion. They used aliases of course.

"It's quite messy." Tweedle Dum admitted.

"You didn't watch it devour that girl did you?"

"Of course not. I just. Well, should we be doing this?"

"We give these children the most humane death we can." Tweedle Dee worried that his friend was wavering. Their job was all that kept the human race from extinction.

They kidnapped girls and dragged them from their families. Then these girls were injected with drugs to interfere with memory so that if they escaped they would never find their way home. As a side effect, these same drugs induced vivid hallucinations.

All so they could be fed to these creatures. Monsters that only allowed humanity to exist so long as they were fed human children. This might be grim work. But it was sacred grim work.

"I wonder what her final thoughts were?" Tweedle Dum seemed to have calmed a bit.

"How should I know?" Tweedle Dee commented. "She was probably wandering lost in a wonderland of her mind's creation."

"How long till we get our next shipment?"

Tweedle Dum had fully recovered. He acted all worried after every job. This emotional back and forth was just another day for these two. Long ago Tweedle Dee stopped worrying about what happened to these children. The entire world's survival was at stake.

Alice Falls Into Wonderland by Ross Ellison

To that end, he would continue to kidnap children if that is what it took to save the world. Luckily, there were so many children to choose from. And in rich and affluent neighborhoods, parents let their kids play by themselves. These were the perfect targets.

"Anyway, something has been on my mind." Tweedle Dum sounded just fine. Did he have a genuine question now?

"Why do the creatures want the girls to be called Alice?"

"How should I know?" Tweedle Dee shrugged. "These beings are far above our comprehension. Just so long as the drugs allow us to convince them that they have always been named Alice it shouldn't matter why."

"Well. If we are serving them to keep humanity safe, the least we can do is wonder why they do what they do."

"Those sorts of questions get people killed in this line of work. Come on." Tweedle Dee scoffed. "Let's smoke and take five before our next job."

ROSS ELLISON

Ross Ellison is an Author, Entertainer, Video Game Streamer, and All Around Menace to Society. Living in Orlando, Florida he currently is working on the next two novels in his Search For Eden Series which the End of Utopia Anthology serves as an introduction for. He also is working on a Post Apocalyptic Series with the working title of "Earth Everafter"

University of Central Florida's Online Publication Imprint selected his work for publication . He works at an online publication called BentoByte where one can find reviews on Anime and Video Games as well as articles on pop culture. Ross pesters society at large with his political commentary.

Writers of Central Florida or Thereabouts selected Ross as a featured Speaker. He is known as "the writer who always goes first" at the many open mics hosted by the organization. Odyssey Orlando has also published multiple pieces of work by Ross.

Whether through his Dark Fantasy Fiction, or commentary on issues that strike his fancy, Ross strives to entertain and educate audiences. Though his writing may deal with difficult issues, these are the ideas which drive society forward. Braving through his work will reward readers with high entertainment value as well as the potential for learning.

He is always looking for collaborators to aid in his endeavors of bringing his work to life. If you are interested in working with him, or have an idea to pitch, do not hesitate to visit the Collaborations Page

Discover more Demonic Anthologies on Amazon

Demonic Wildlife VOL I

https://books2read.com/DemonicWildlife

You are about to set foot on a bizarre adventure, a funny fantastical one filled with demonic animals. The first few stories are light, more about the giggles, but be warned. As you read further, the dark creepy side will sneak up on you. Within this entertaining tome you will find spiders, snakes, sheep, wolves, manatees, hummingbirds, squirrels, and many more!

Demonic Household VOL II

https://books2read.com/DemonicHousehold

You are traveling into a dark and humorous place. We start you off with light, soft stories, but be warned. You will find yourself falling into the ever darker, gorier, and more demonic stories with each passing page. You may look at your couch, your washer, and even television and wonder if you should be laughing anymore. Will your household turn on you? Keep your Owner's Manuals close by!

Demonic Carnival VOL III

https://books2read.com/DemonicCarnival

You are traveling into a dark and humorous place. We start you off with light, soft stories, but be warned. You will find yourself falling into the ever darker, gorier, and more demonic stories with each passing story. From heartwarming endings to feeling like you just walked out of the Carnival Port-a-potty into another dimension - this collection will leave your mind spinning. The Fried Food stall, the Ferris Wheel, and even that carnival themed hotel in Vegas... all of it will never be the same for you after your visit to the Demonic Carnival. Remember... First Ticket's Free...

Follow us on Facebook at:

www.facebook.com/DemonicAnthologies/

https://www.facebook.com/BattleGoddessPro/

More books from 4 Horsemen Publications

Anthologies & Collections

4HP Anthologies
Teen Angst: Mix Vol. 1
Teen Angst: Mix Vol. 2
My Wedding Date
The Offices of
Supernatural Being
The Sentient Space

Demonic Anthologies
Demonic Wildlife
Demonic Household
Demonic Carnival
Demonic Classics
Demonic Vacations
Demonic Medicine
Demonic Workplace
& more to follow!

XXX- Holiday Collection
Unwrap Me
Stuffing My Stocking
Put a Little Irish in Me

Fantasy, SciFi, & Paranormal Romance

Beau Lake
The Beast Beside Me
The Beast Within Me
Taming the Beast: Novella
The Beast After Me
Charming the Beast: Novella
The Beast Like Me
An Eye for Emeralds
Swimming in Sapphires
Pining for Pearls

Danielle Orsino
Locked Out of Heaven
Thine Eyes of Mercy
From the Ashes
Kingdom Come
Fire, Ice, Acid, & Heart

J.M. Paquette
Klauden's Ring
Solyn's Body
The Inbetween
Hannah's Heart
Call Me Forth
Invite Me In
Keep Me Close

Lyra R. Saenz
Prelude
Falsetto in the
Woods: Novella
Ragtime Swing
Sonata
Song of the Sea
The Devil's Trill
Bercuese
To Heal a Songbird
Ghost March
Nocturne

T.S. Simons
Antipodes
The Liminal Space
Ouroboros
Caim
Sessrúmnir

Valerie Willis
Cedric: The Demonic Knight
Romasanta: Father of
Werewolves
The Oracle: Keeper of the
Gaea's Gate
Artemis: Eye of Gaea
King Incubus: A New Reign

V.C. Willis
The Prince's Priest
The Priest's Assassin
The Assassin's Saint

DISCOVER MORE AT 4HORSEMENPUBLICATIONS.COM